David Burt started writing aged 80, using his experience working in various jobs and businesses—from his start on a building site, through National Service in the RAF, a national bank, selling and marketing and operational management before becoming the CEO of a major international manufacturing company supplying the aerospace industry. His short stories are all based on incidences that he has observed, or in which he has been involved.

Dedication

Sally-Anne, my daughter, who encouraged me into writing. My wife, Sonia, daughters, Samantha and Katherine, son, Charles, and my ten grandchildren.

David Burt

ALL SORTS AND SURPRISES

AUSTIN MACAULEY PUBLISHERS™

LONDON • CAMBRIDGE • NEW YORK • SHARJAH

A CIP catalogue record for this title is available from the British Library.

ISBN 9781788238731 (Paperback)
ISBN 9781788238748 (Hardback)
ISBN 9781788238755 (E-Book)

www.austinmacauley.com

First Published (2018)
Austin Macauley Publishers Ltd™
25 Canada Square
Canary Wharf
London
E14 5LQ

Acknowledgements

Janet, my PA, who has typed every word I have written and done it with much patience!

Contents

The Eyes and Ears of the Company

Lucy Dewson placed the tray with its load of four mugs of tea, two with, two without sugar, and a plate generously overfilled with chocolate digestive biscuits, on the table before enquiring, "Now, gentlemen, which of you were with sugar?" She dealt the mugs according to the hand signals before adding, "And please help yourself to the biscuits."

Lucy retreated to her desk at the front of the reception area where she could survey the front door and, if she chose, keep an eye on the four customers visiting the car hire company. There was a gap she could adjust in the heavy curtains behind her seat so she could hear their discussions as they relaxed with the tea and biscuits, falsely feeling secure in their comfortable surrounds before their meeting with the Company Manager to negotiate their white van hire agreements.

As usual, Lucy took note of several of their comments until her internal phone buzzed and the Sales Director asked her if she would mind escorting the Lockwood Delivery people up to his office.

Lucy confirmed her hair was to her liking and her lipstick in place in her mirror, before asking the visiting business group to accompany her to the first floor office door, emblazoned with a brass nameplate, 'Walter B. Bourne F.Inst.M'.

Tapping on the door and hearing a loud 'Enter', she did so and introduced the business men before she took her leave as they settled themselves in front of Walter B. Bourne's considerable desk, enlivened by a framed photograph of a youthful W.B.B. in leathers sitting, somewhat uncomfortably, on a Matchless Twin motorcycle that he claimed showed his 'grassroots' interest in the motor trade.

Lucy walked down the corridor to the end door which was unmarked and walked in without knocking.

William McDonnell was sitting at an over cluttered desk, half the size of W.B.B.s.

Lucy went across the office to the water dispenser and enquired if William wanted a refill. Receiving a negative response from the CEO, who was sucking on his biro anxiously whilst he continued to stare into his computer screen, she filled a glass for herself and sat down in the chair at the end of his table.

"Well," said William, "what do you think?"

Lucy reflected, staring at the picture of William with his wife and four children on the beach at Morecambe Bay on the wall.

"They have a quote in from Minehead Motors. They mentioned Frank Blake who you know is the CEO and they are being led in their thinking by the accountant, Terry Armstrong, who doesn't say a lot but when he does, they all listen."

Lucy thought quietly for a moment. "The CEO, Hardcastle, is not strong. He is unsure and worried. I sense the company has to get the lease arrangements for the five delivery vans right or they are going to struggle this year to fulfil their contracts but their profit margins are minimal I gathered from the accountant's comments."

Lucy continued, "My feeling is if we don't make a concession and drop the price below the existing contract, we are going to lose this one and that will be the third contract we have lost this quarter and we know what Ford will think about that. I don't trust W.W.B. to bombast the accountant into agreement. You know what a buffoon he can be when he's rattled."

W.McD rocked his head back and forth sadly. "I know, I know, but he knows as well as everybody we are going to be crossed off Ford's list as main distributor if we cannot improve our figures. What do you suggest I might do with these guys while we still have a chance?"

Lucy was immediately positive. "I strongly suggest you separate the CEO from the rest. Get him in here, give him an assurance he will get a special discount because of his importance. You will have to cut back our percentage from Fords, perhaps three percent, but it has to be worth that to hold the agency. Then offer him your tickets to Ascot for him and his wife, you've been lots of times. I think he will like to get one over his accountant. Help him show he can get a result when he negotiates."

"Thanks, Lucy. Thank goodness we have someone on the front desk who can work out some practical options for the company. Right, I will go down and break up W.W.B's little party and get Mr Hardcastle in for a private cup of tea and a chat and see what I can do."

A week later the CEO called a senior managers' meeting with Lucy sitting by his side as the little group of managers trooped in to the boardroom.

"Well, everybody, good news. Advance Van Hire have been able to hold the Lockwood Delivery account for their vans for another year. We have had to drop our commission by 3% to do so but the important thing was to retain our agency with Ford, and as you all know they are threatening us with a sub-agency status if we cannot increase our take of hire vans, and we simply have to bring in every opportunity."

W.McD continued as he looked around at the managers. "I should add we would not have been in this position if we had not had Lucy's smart help in preparing the way to convince Lockwood Delivery to stay with us."

Everyone looked at Lucy, who looked down at her shoes.

The CEO continued. "Lucy is going to continue to work closely with me as we try every way we can to bring in some new customers for the Ford vans. I don't care if it's only one or two, they will all add up. So let's go to work. Sales, sales, sales. W.B.B. could you stay a minute, I would like to get an idea of your marketing focus and Lucy I would like you to hear what Walter has to say."

Within the hour the Sales Office was filled with anxiety and the sounds of wheeling and dealing as the Sales Director and his team focused on every enquiry they could for leasing of vans.

Lucy now was more and more seen as the 'eyes and ears' of the sales effort, listening and watching when she had a potential customer in the reception room feeding off her tea and biscuits. She had even extended this service to sandwiches and light ale for the over-lunch negotiations, when she arranged them in the company's 'comfortable private room' in the most advantageous way to allow her to hear as the customers chatted over the negotiation offers being made.

It was in this way that Lucy's instinct for what was going on below the surface was most tested.

Some few days after the CEO's meeting, W.B.B. came down to inform Lucy, "Our Receptionist," as he rather disparagingly liked to introduce her, that he had three business men coming in that morning. She should not sign them in as the deal had to be 'hush, hush'. They were coming in to see him to conclude a deal he had 'as good as done' for six top rate Ford rental white vans for twelve months.

"Most unusually," as he explained to Lucy, "a cash deal if we can get the vans for next week and a year's rental paid up front. I am working on the delivery now so give them your best tea and biscuit smile when they get here at ten o'clock."

Sure enough precisely at ten, three men in dark overcoats entered reception and came up to Lucy's desk. The leader, a tanned Italian looking man with beautiful teeth, enquired in perfect English if they could see Mr Walter Bourne with a smile that did not engage his eyes. "We are expected," he said.

Lucy asked if they would care to sit while she contacted Mr Bourne and invited them to take tea. All, as it turned out, without sugar!

Lucy fixed the tea and complementary biscuits, calling W.W.B. advising him that his customers had arrived.

W.W.B. asked Lucy to hold them in reception as Ford's Distribution Manager was trying to adjust schedules to get the vehicles for the following Friday.

Half an hour later W.W.B. bounced into the reception ante-room beaming at his customers, as he informed them that the six transit vans would be delivered on Thursday and ready for them on Friday morning at eight as they had required.

Lucy, hovering in the background, observed the knowing exchange between the three before an envelope, thick with fifty pound notes, was passed to W.W.B. and the senior man gave a private address in South Croydon, rather than the address of a company, although that did not seem to bother W.W.B. who was enthusiastically gathering the hire form, having counted the bank banded bundles of fifty pound notes, beaming as he did so.

W.W.B. positively bowed his way out of the reception ante-room as he craved the three overcoats' indulgence for, "just a few more moments," whilst he went to authorise the rental agreements.

Lucy retreated to her seat in reception and had scarcely seated herself before she heard a mobile phone ring.

From her seat of observation she slid the folds of the heavy curtain a fraction and saw the over coated back of the customer, with the beautiful smile, holding a mobile phone clamped to his ear.

"Yes, yes," he was saying impatiently. "Nothing has changed, the vans are sorted. No, we will pick them up. Just make doubly sure your people are in place at each site as we arranged. Of course, we will dump them when we do the change over to the other wheels. Look, I can't talk anymore."

Lucy sat and thought for some time after the three, with their signed agreements, had left the office and W.W.B. has rushed up to the CEO's office to give him the good news.

Finally, she called Pauline, a member of her badminton club who managed the canteen in the local Police Station.

"Pauline, this is a funny one. I feel there's something wrong with a six-white van hire for next Friday and I just wondered if you could chat to one of the CID girls," as she went on to explain her concerns.

In no time at all a plain clothes CID officer was in reception asking for Lucy and with a cup of tea and her confirmation that their conversation would be shared in complete confidence, he explained there was 'chatter' about a possible job next week involving six villains, known more for their muscles than their minds.

In view of the six-van upfront payment and specific timing demands, which as the CID officer explained, "Might be to avoid having to steal suitable vehicles to move heavy equipment, or the result of a burglary of some sort, would the company co-operate by having tracker devices fitted in the vans the night before they were to leave the company?"

Lucy explained the request and the background to the horrified CEO.

"If Ford hear about this we will be off their agents' list in a second. Oh goodness what can I tell the bank, our overdraft's touching the ceiling now. Where will we pick up vans… our name will be mud in the trade."

Lucy stopped him short.

"William, stop prattling, we are to co-operate with the CID. Leave that to me. Tell no one, least of all W.W.B, he will just have a heart attack."

At eight o'clock the following Thursday evening, Lucy with the key and CID operatives, were fitting a tiny magnetic tracking device into the engine bay of each of the white vans.

On Friday morning as close to ten o'clock as makes no difference, six Post Office weekly security delivery vehicles throughout the county were stopping at Post Offices behind inconveniently parked white Ford transit vans whilst trying to make their delivery of cash containers.

Each white van driver and his burly assistant found themselves surrounded by a squad of policemen the moment they left their white van.

Back in the company just after Lucy had been phoned to be told of the successful outcome by the CID officer, without passing the news to anyone, she phoned her long standing friend in the Ford Distribution department and explained to the Distribution Manager's Secretary how the company had saved Ford from the serious embarrassment of being associated with a series of Post Office burglaries by Advance Hire company working with the CID and Lucy hoped this would count in their favour.

A week later in William's office, the CEO brandished a letter about his head excitedly as he told the company team.

"It's confirmed the continuation of the company's agency agreement with Ford, with the promise of an area launch of the new transit model in the spring, financed by Ford, here on our premises."

The CEO steadied up to say, "All this is down to Lucy's special skills and I offered her the job of Marketing Manager, but she turned me down saying she likes doing what she has always done for us. Needless to say I have given her a substantial rise anyway!"

Everyone cheered and clapped as Lucy sat looking down at her shoes.

Sleepless Nights

"Why me, what have I done to deserve all this pressure?"

"Just a minute dear, let me get the kids off to get the school bus."

Duncan sat at the breakfast table staring morosely at the remnants in his cereal bowl, his hand around his mug of tea.

Margaret bustled back into the kitchen, having had a few moments to ensure the children had their homework books and sports gear as they clattered off to the bus stop giving her time to consider the anxious, even depressed, state of her husband in the kitchen.

"Now then Duncan it really is not all bad, you know your dad's going to get the best treatment and he is a tough old stick. You've said so dozens of times and he is well able to look after himself now your Mum's gone. And the new responsibilities with the job, you know you can get on top of that. That Mr Hetherington told you how much the company value your knowledge, and let's face it we can do with the money with Terry growing up so quickly."

"I know, I know, but I just don't know if I can deal with all the pressure of work. I've got months of work to sort out that team as well as look after my own lot. Now I will have to go in regular to see my dad's doing the right things and I don't know anything about the prostate cancer treatment, or the effect of the treatment, whatever that is, and you know I haven't really got over Mum going that quickly. It would help if I could sleep a bit better."

Duncan held his head in his hands with his arms on the kitchen table.

"Oh come on now, you are the family rock and you've got to tidy up and go to work. I will look on the iPad to find out more about this prostate cancer treatment and so when you've popped in to see your dad on the way home tonight I will be able to give you a better picture of things."

Later tidying Terry's bedroom, which gave the impression that a tornado had passed through, Margaret had the opportunity to worry more about her husband's state of mind. She thought again he had been something of a 'mother's boy'. An only child in a very caring family, excessively proud of their son's degree in Engineering and his determined focus upon a 'good' career.

Margaret smiled as she remembered her mother-in-law's not very subtle interview with her, when Duncan had finally announced he was going to invite her to be his wife. She realised, as she moved about the house tidying up, that perhaps unwittingly her role had moved into a version of her mother-in-law's relationship with her son.

Supporting, encouraging, guiding and, Margaret thought, *perhaps I have shielded him a bit too much from the realities of life, playing to his tidy organised mind even when events, as now, require a bit of a reaction out of the ordinary.*

In his office Duncan was trying to focus on the two men and a woman engineering group he had just inherited as they sat tensely opposite him. Social chitchat at the best of times was not Duncan's strong card and this morning he was wishing he was elsewhere.

"Er, I expect you wonder why the CEO has transferred you to my section. Well I'm not sure either."

If he had expected some sign of amusement Duncan certainly did not get it and so after a pause he continued.

"Well your work on Applied Process is close to my team and I expect the CEO thought we could speed projects up a bit."

Without any reaction from the three in front of him, Duncan was forced into a new tack to engage some sort of response.

"Now, Graham," he said, looking at his note from the HR Manager. "You seem to have been in the company the longest. Perhaps you could give us your views on the change."

Graham shifted in his overalls and adjusted the spectacles on his nose, finally saying awkwardly.

"Blow if I know what the point is we were alright working with Mr March. He let us get on with it."

This last comment was matched by head nodding from the other two.

"Now we dunno what to fink…"

Following a few more less than informative comments Duncan disbanded the meeting with the comment.

"As soon as I get time I will come down and see what each of you is doing but in the meantime just carry on as before."

Pressed as he was Duncan realised this had not been a successful first meeting and this was on his mind as he took his customary detour that evening to arrive at his father's house.

Putting his key into the front door, Duncan stopped for a moment to reflect that their normal cup of tea and discussion on the situation in the county cricket match was unlikely to suit the discussion today, with the arrival of the news his father had telephoned him about yesterday of the GP's confirmation that his father had prostate cancer and the need for immediate treatment.

"Hi, dad," Duncan called as he went towards the kitchen where he was pleased to see his father at the kitchen table as usual reading the evening paper, the teapot on the Aga.

"Hallo, son, had a good day with your new people?"

"Well not really but you know they need to get used to the change and to me. Anyway, how are you feeling, that's much more important."

"Same as usual, Doc says I will feel tired when they start the radiation but not to worry. What do you think happens when I do start this treatment?"

Duncan floundered through tea and confusion, admitting that he had very little idea about the treatment to kill off the cancer cells. Leaving his father with the encouragement that when he came over tomorrow he hoped he would have a bit more information.

A few weeks later with the treatment beginning to take its toll on his father and the new unit deliberately trying to maintain their independence, avoiding Duncan's attempts to combine their activities with his original group, his nerves not being helped at home by his son's lack of attention to his schoolwork which Margaret patiently explained as the natural arrival of a hormone change that she insisted was influencing all forms of attitude to 'discipline'. However, his son's disruptive behaviour was causing Duncan more stress, whatever the reasons.

All these events were bearing down on Duncan to the point that his wife made an appointment for him to visit his doctor to get some help for his sleepless nights and daily stress.

Duncan was by no means a regular visitor to Dr Clark's surgery and despite the doctor's notes prepared by his medical assistant, following the discussion she had on the phone with Margaret, he found Duncan's reticence difficult to deal with in the short period scheduled for the patient's visit.

Finally, Dr Clark said.

"Look, Mr Holmes I am giving you the address of a Stress and Cancer Information Centre here in the town, quite close to your office. The people that run it are all volunteers. Nobody gets paid but everyone has been through difficult times and they have been trained to offer support and help. The comfortable and relaxed house they have is organised so that you can drop in as often as you like, have a cup of tea and chat with someone who has been through stressful times and understands. I think it would help you get back in balance and then we can make an appointment for a month's time when I think it will be easier for us to decide if we can help by having a little clearer picture. In the meantime I am giving you a prescription for some sleeping pills."

A week later in his lunch break, Duncan took the short walk to a cul-de-sac with its row of Victorian town houses until he came to the steps of No. 7.

Duncan saw the discreet sign, Hemsley Drop-in Centre in the window, the only thing differentiating the three-storey house from the others in the road.

Duncan hesitated, hand on the three step iron handrail, about to turn away when the front door opened and a middle-aged lady with a cheery smile, neat in a twin-set outfit and with an identification badge said.

"Do come in, you really are most welcome."

And she came down the steps proffering her hand.

"I am Mary," leading Duncan into the hallway where she got him to sign in. "Health & Safety you know," she said turning to smile at him, before leading him into what Duncan saw must have been the front room, comfortably furnished with sofas and chairs, with a small tea bar and table loaded with biscuits and cakes.

As Duncan looked around the room where several people were sitting talking quietly together, Mary enquired.

"Would you like a cup of tea before I introduce you to Gwen, she knows everything about the place and likes to talk to everyone who pops in for the first time."

Duncan found himself with a cup of tea and sitting with Gwen who immediately set Duncan at his ease. She explained how the drop-in centre worked and at the same time, without seeming to do so, got Duncan to explain all his concerns and misgivings, all without him feeling awkward or embarrassed to be talking to a complete stranger about such personal matters.

Telling Margaret about the visit that evening and explaining he had an appointment for a second lunch time visit in a few days, Duncan was further encouraged to find his wife was very supportive of the project and for the first time since Dr Clark had given him the sleeping pills, he did not take one that night and managed to sleep through the night without dreams of his struggles at work or finding himself standing in front of the school with the headmaster admonishing him.

Over the next three weeks, Duncan visited the drop-in centre counsellor several times. She helped him by preparing a detail of the effects on the daily life of an older man undergoing the kind of treatment his father was receiving. She also listened carefully to Duncan as he gradually opened up giving background detail about his struggles and stress.

At his next visit she said, "Duncan, I really do feel I have the picture of the way you see things and I can understand your concerns and I think I have a plan which I am going to suggest to you that I think might help."

This said she laid out in some detail her suggested programme.

As a result, on the very next Saturday morning Duncan took his son to meet his grandfather, a procedure he had avoided since his father had started his treatment, partially he now realised to penalise his son for his somewhat irritating behaviour at home and partially as he thought his father would not want to be bothered by his grandson when he was not feeling well.

The reunion meeting was joyful from both parties and Duncan was surprised to hear his father going through the detail of the treatment with his grandson and how he was feeling. The lad responded to this confidence by telling his grandfather he had been 'got at' by an older boy who 'fancied' a girl, Sue, a pupil in the sister girls' school who he had had a first tentative one-to-one meeting with in the Costa coffee shop and who he hoped would become a more regular date. This was to the irritation of the older boy who had been trying to date Sue for some time.

All information that Duncan had no inclination of until he sat silently listening at the kitchen table as the two shared their experiences.

With a promise to be back the following Saturday, Duncan drove his new cheerful and chatty son home and when he introduced the potential next step in 'The Plan' without indicating it was anything of the sort, his son simply said. "Yep right, OK sure."

A week later in the half term, Duncan introduced his son as, "visiting to get a little experience," in his weekly rather stilted technical update meeting with the three members of his new team.

The meeting began with Duncan having to probe carefully for any detail of their programmes in the week. Constantly trying to find some way of linking their equipment development with the system work in which his own team were involved.

Matters drifted on with his son listening intently, until one of the team mentioned they were considering linking two of their experimental units by fibre optic cable than copper cable.

At this point Duncan's son abruptly joined in the conversation.

"I'm working on a fibre optic cable project at school. We have a visiting student at Imperial College doing his Ph.D., with this as his research paper. He's a great guy and has chosen me as the group liaison."

Duncan sat back in his chair amazed at the news.

His son continued. "We are seeing how lower the signal attention is with fibre optic cable. You know, higher band with more data."

At this point the new team were all focused upon Duncan's son.

"No, go on, how interesting. We are just looking into the fibre optic cable options," said the three all talking at once.

"We were shown last week just how effective the fibre optic cable is in avoiding stray interference," replied Duncan's son.

Later in the day after Duncan's son had disappeared with the new team, the meeting reconvened when Duncan was told that.

"If we do use a fibre optic link we should be able to interface the two unit's projects into the one programme."

An atmosphere so different from the past, that Duncan found it difficult to explain to the drop-in centre counsellor the dramatic improvement. She just smiled and said.

"I hope you will drop in and have a cup of tea regularly. I would love to know how things progress for you and your father and of course you 'new' group at work, and most of all now you have established a whole new relationship with your son."

On his follow up visit to the surgery, Dr Clark simply said.

"Well, it sounds to me as if you have dealt with your stress problems very well and you certainly don't need any more help from me. I only wish I could get such a good result with all my patients!"

The Retiring Man

It was not so much that Harold Painter underestimated his abilities but rather more that he never thought about them without his wife's guidance and direction, although shaving that morning he looked at himself and knew that even without her, he would have to decide what he would do next.

If only Hilda had not passed away, thought Harold, *she would have given me a clear plan of action from the day after I retire from the bank.*

Looking bleakly at himself in the mirror, Harold wiped soap off his face and finally addressed the thought that his pedestrian days travelling from junior clerk to senior clerk in the bank were coming to an end.

Harold sighed deeply. Without Hilda's direction how could he find some activity to compensate for the daily discipline and comfort of the No. 31 bus and the bank's all-consuming rules and procedures before he returned to No. 26 Acacia Avenue and his carefully organised life overseen in every way by Hilda? He had tried when he received the formal notice of his retirement date from the Personnel Department to consider his options, but the future seemed terrifying to Harold, causing him to have recurring nightmares.

Harold had purchased a book from the 'self-help' section of Waterstones bookshop entitled *A Guide for the smooth transition into Retirement* and despite assiduously ploughing through the chapters one after another, only putting down the book on his bedside table at 9.45 p.m. to turn off the light, if anything the 'Self-help book' increased his anxiety, with such chapters with charts for 'self-measurement to prepare yourself for the retirement phase of your life'!

Testing everything from the nutritious intake of his daily food to levels of alcohol and other stimuli, Harold baulked at the section requiring box ticking on his response to sexual stimulation of partners of either gender. He also found the chapter requiring his values on the relationships he experienced at a wide range of clubs from golf to political and cultural groups, where the reader might increase his or her involvement, of no value at all as he held no membership cards.

An issue that bothered Harold and came up in one form of disturbing dream segment or another, was the thought that without the casual interface he had daily with members of the bank staff, many over several years, he would become even more lonely and isolated than he was since Hilda had departed.

Returning each evening to an unlit and unprepared house had forcibly brought loneliness like a blanket of misery into his life, a situation which was about to get worse, forcing Harold to decide he had to act to prepare himself for his impending retirement date.

Therefore, like it or not, he had had to make a decision over the path he had to take and this, for the first time in his life, it had to be done all on his own.

Previous paths had been selected by his dominant mother, including his choice, not that he had one, of his job in the bank and his wife, Hilda, who his mother met in the library and decided she would make a suitable wife.

The bank had directed every step of his modest career and his wife had directed every other aspect of his life until her quite unexpected demise on a Friday morning when the grocery delivery driver had come to the house with the weekly delivery. His procedure was to tap, as quickly as it was possible on the back door, open it and call softly, "Are you there, Mrs Painter?" in the hope he could slip in and have the grocery order on the table and slip out without having to face Mrs Painter, who would if she caught him, as she usually did, go through each item on the bill, frequently weighing loose items to ensure the accuracy of the delivery before he could escape to continue his round.

On this morning he found Mrs Painter sitting bolt upright in her wheel back kitchen chair, staring at him with unseeing eyes, an unnerving experience for the young man who had the presence of mind to call an ambulance, when matters were taken out of his hands.

Now, only a few weeks later in the bank, to Harold's considerable surprise the bank's security guard came over as Harold took his morning tea break in the canteen and unceremoniously dumped himself down with his sandwich pack and the Daily Star newspaper on the table next to him.

It was well known that Harold liked to sit quietly on his own with his tea, no sugar, and the *Daily Mail* paper. One of his few indulgencies which he could get away with without Hilda being aware of his pleasure for reading a paper that Hilda regarded as a *'common little rag with left wing tendencies and encouraged people to gamble excessively on racehorses.'*

Harold shifted himself slightly sideways as William Dormitt, known generally as 'Bill Doorstop' as a result of his security role at the banks' front door, leaned his considerable girth over the table towards him.

"Well now, Mr Painter, what are you going to do with yourself when you leave us?" enquired Bill Doorstop with a smile on his face.

This question was totally surprising to Harold on two counts. In the several years they had known each other, the only discussion had been of the 'good morning, 'good evening you will need your umbrella tonight, Mr Painter' exchange without a hint of interest by either party to explore any wider conversational issues.

"I expect when you have more time on your hands you will be spending it with old friends?"

The nature of Bill Doorstop's interest forced a response from Harold who replied.

"Well, I haven't decided yet but I expect I will give one or two old school friends a call."

He replied rather defensively, surprising himself as he did so as he had given no thought to this possible line of action.

"Good idea, good idea," said Bill Doorstop, adding gloomily, "I wish my retirement was coming up, no such luck. I have years to do at the bank before I get a pension."

The idea of calling up one or two old school contacts kept to the forefront of Harold's mind as he wended his way home on the No. 31 bus, stopping only to pick up a 'take-away' meal from the corner shop, under the watchful gaze of Gladys Fulsome, the proprietor, who had once been heard telling a lady customer as he reached into the freezer display for a single portion of veal and ham pie, 'such a shame he has no one to look after him now, poor little soul.'

The following day at the bank, Harold had a shortlist of three pupils who he remembered as being of 'like spirit' at avoiding games and much school work as possible. Firmly gripping the lip balm tube in his pocket, his way of steeling himself, Harold called his old junior public school in the depth of Dorset, using the 'Hatchlands Annual Report' that he and every other ex-student received each year, a copy of which he kept out of a sense of loyalty and with a slight hope that someone would ask him what school he had been to. No one ever did!

Harold phoned the school number whilst looking at the photograph of the school secretary on the inside page before asking to speak to Miss Patricia Pembury, explaining he was an old boy and to encourage the transfer he said, "I am calling from the A.M.P. Bank, Head Office." A trick he had picked up years before to elevate the importance of his call in the hope, generally resulting, that he would get informed attention rather than his enquiry being dealt with by some disinterested operator.

Harold was however somewhat surprised when he was put through instantly.

"How nice of you to call back, this is Patricia Pembury, we so want a senior bank official like yourself, one of our respected old boys, to talk to the school at the end of term and the Headmaster and the school directors would be really delighted if you could talk for a few minutes at our end of term day so that the boys could be inspired by hearing someone who had been at the school and had achieved great success in the banking world. We will, of course, send a car to bring you down and have booked a suite at the Grand Hotel in Barchester."

By now despite the torrent of information Harold had worked out this was a case of mistaken identity.

Miss Pembury continued unabated.

"We were so worried that we would not be able to get a banker to come down. We had tried several of you old boys; several could not make the fifteenth of next month. Indeed, your call represents our last chance. Thank you, thank you so much for helping the school out."

Harold had prepared himself several times to explain his reason for calling but there was no space in the flow of words from Miss Pembury for him to inject the purpose in calling.

Miss Pembury carried on speaking.

"Mr Painter… may I call you Harold? My assistant has just passed me your school record and I see you were an exemplary student quietly pursuing your studies with us, without causing the kind of disruption as so many of our students give the staff today. An ideal background so that now you have achieved such success in the banking world at the end of your career you can inspire a new generation of our pupils to follow your lead."

Faced with this accolade of success, false as it was, Harold found himself basking in the warmth of the words unique to his ears and when Miss Pembury finally stopped to draw breath, Harold was able to mumble, "Delighted to help."

Personal telephone numbers exchanged with the promise of a detail for the travel and five star accommodations to follow, Harold sank back in his chair in a state of anxiety and suppressed excitement, never before having received an accolade let alone a compliment declaring his success in any field of his uneventful life.

The retirement dinner hosted by a very recently appointed junior regional director, who managed to refer to Harold as Harry, sitting with a dozen colleagues from the office dragooned into the dinner, all of whom would rather be watching TV or up the pub, than listening to the young director droning on about service and credit to the bank when he clearly had no more personal recollection of Harold's time than three paragraphs on a paper from the Personnel Department.

Harold had at least made some attempt to prepare a response bringing in the names of several of the bank's luminaries who he had met at one time or another. He was motivated by the thought that the notes might help in a name dropping way when he was addressing his old school pupils.

The bank's retirement evening was somewhat stilted, stuffy and hurried but Harold managed to be courteous and grateful when he accepted his leaving gift of a figurative side table lamp, a gilded plaster cast of two entwined figures gaudily decorated who in the rather dim lighting of the function room gave the impression they were performing a complex sex act. The lamp had been donated by the Personnel Department at the last minute when it was realised no staff collection for Harold had been arranged and had been found in a store cupboard that had been gifted some years before but considered as a totally unsuitable wedding gift for one of the secretaries, even though she had been known to be adventurous!

Harold found it quite easy preparing himself for the school event to claim he had a liking for the generous gift, claiming it would have a special place in his 'new' life and remain as a reminder of his 'close' colleagues in the bank.

The effusiveness of his thanks surprised several of his colleagues. One or two detected a subtle irony in his comments which caused considerable surprise in the after dinner discussions.

"Didn't know he had it in him, sneaky old bugger laughing at us there in his booth."

Harold found the limousine trip down to Dorset most satisfying. The driver's courteous attention and the pre-arranged stop for lunch did much to dispel his queasy feeling about delivering his fifty times written speech to the boys, their parents and teachers the next day.

The arrival at the prestigious hotel in Barchester was again very gratifying to Harold who was totally unused to polite subservience and attention to his every whim.

In his spacious hotel suite he found an envelope with a message suggesting he might like to take the short walk through the park to the school to remind him of the direction for the following day, together with a list of the senior staff and directors he would be meeting at the event.

Soon after changing into comfortable attire, Harold made his way through the hotel foyer and bowed down the entrance steps by the doorman who could easily have been a sergeant in the Grenadier Guards.

The walk across the open park and through a screen of neatly cut privet hedges was as he remembered things fifty years before, but entering the rest of the school grounds the view before him had changed dramatically. Now new buildings existed where the tennis courts had once been, an area to avoid at all costs.

Turning first left and then right, he still saw no way to the front entrance and in some desperation he approached a small boy wandering with his face to the ground, hands in pockets, who might offer Harold some information.

"Young man, could you direct me to the school entrance please."

The young pupil visibly jerked himself back from where his mind was leading him, looking thoroughly surprised by being challenged in this way.

"Yes, sir, if you wouldn't mind following me," he finally said, withdrawing his hands from his trouser pockets.

Harold realised an explanation was necessary to steady the boy.

"I am here for the finals day event tomorrow as I am an old boy of the school. What's your name?"

"Gillesby, sir, 3B."

"Oh 3B, that's the very class I started in when I came to the school." Harold nearly said forty-two years ago but caught himself and added, "A few years ago."

"Now this is the end of your first year, I expect you have just had your end of year report and how did you do?"

Gillesby scuffed the ground with the toe of his shoe and said.

"Not very well, sir."

Looking to cheer the boy up, Harold said, "I know how you are feeling. I had a poor report at the end of my first year and my mother was not very pleased." An understatement Harold thought.

"Why have you come back then?" Gillesby asked in some surprise.

This was a question that Harold was quite unable to answer as Gillesby had stopped walking and was now staring up at his face in surprise.

"Did you become one of our Star pupils later?"

"Well no, no not at all but your school secretary, Miss Pembury, has asked me to come down and talk to all you boys, because I work in a big bank."

"Golly, but I suppose you are really only going to be talking to all the bright boys here and I'm not very bright and I don't know how to tell my mother and father about my report tomorrow when they come to collect me."

Tears ran down Gillesby's cheeks and Harold, without thinking, handed Gillesby his handkerchief instinctively knowing that the boy would not have one, a situation he would have been in all those years ago.

They walked on in silence until they rounded the science block and saw the entrance steps and doors. Harold stopped, suddenly clear for the first time what had to be done tomorrow.

"Listen young Gillesby, I had a miserable time here too and I am going to talk about that to boys like you, not just the bright ones and I will see if I can make it easier for your parents to accept your end of year report tomorrow."

Back in the hotel suite later, Harold discarded his speech notes and spent some time preparing for his talk to the boys and their parents the next day.

The school hall was packed with boys, their parents and the teaching staff and school trustees, all sitting in tiered ranks beneath the frowning faces of the luminaries whose paintings adorned the walls into the high vaulted ceilings.

The headmaster had beamed benignly to the left and right as he informed his audience of the great successes the school had achieved in every department of academic endeavour during the year, highlighting with arms upraised, the classic scholars whose entry into Oxford had been achieved on the back of winning bursaries.

He droned on to achievements in the field, on the river and courts where school athletes had 'once again' achieved ringing successes in their various areas.

Before sitting down to the comforting applause of the pupils and parents relieved that their investment, despite the increase in fees, had at least been spent with some hope of return, the Headmaster swept his hand to the right towards Harold, who was perched uncomfortably in the middle of the row of Governors on the stage.

"And today," said the Headmaster, "we are privileged to have with us a distinguished old boy, Mr Harold Painter, senior executive at the A.M.P. Bank who will address us all…, Mr Painter."

Harold had discarded any thought of reading a speech in his hotel room the night before and in doing so he was pleased to feel the weight of Hilda's presence slip from his shoulders.

He strode purposely to the lectern, almost bouncing in his enthusiasm to deliver his message to the expectant throng.

Harold paused, looking across the sea of faces feeling for the first time at ease with himself.

"I would like to explain before I begin," he said, "today I am going to address those boys, and their parents, who are not high academic achievers, who do not excel in sport or in cultural matters, who worry day by day what new challenges will have to be faced."

The look of stony surprise on Miss Pembury's face during Harry's rousing address was markedly softened by the end when the audience's warm and continuous applause swept the hall.

Harold, standing at the lectern with the applause sweeping around him, spotted little Gillesby who had stood tall from his seat and having caught Harold's eye, raised a thumbs up to his own family success.

Harold knew then he had found his own new path.

Later still after a luncheon with the distinguished guests, the Chairman of Governors drew Harold to one side to enquire if he would have time to become a governor and attend the regular meetings and events 'to use' as the Chairman explained 'his special skills and experience to help the school?'

Harold accepted without a moment's thought.

Breaking the Habit

Harry left his elderly grey mini car close to the railings in the van yard, exactly at 6.00 a.m. by the same rail section as he had the day before. Indeed, the year before or had he given the process any thought, the same rail section he had left his well-polished little car each working day for the last twenty years.

Harry did not think about his working day routine as he walked to his company van in slot number One, precisely where he had left it at one o'clock the previous day after his delivery shift. In fact, he was not thinking about anything except the van keys in his right trouser pocket, the same company uniform trousers he wore every day for work.

Harry unlocked his company van and walked to the side door of the long factory building where, had he considered it, the sweet smell of cooking bakeries was filling the air. He tugged open the door and entered the depot, busy with white coated, white hatted and hair netted workers, collecting an array of bakeries from ovens and placing them with their paper cups on to wooden slatted trays.

Harry, walked to Station One, clearly identified with a numbered card and his name, ten trays awaited his six o'clock arrival. As always Harry gave no thought to the process and he began to transport each tray with its range of cakes, buns, tarts and rolls of every filling and description at a steady pace into his van. Fitting each tray on to its slide in the order he would be delivering them to the cake shops on his round.

Never once did Harry glance at his watch or the clock on the bakery wall. He knew by habit exactly where he was in the order of the day's events. He did give a courtesy nod to the Supervisor, who nodded back, neither spoke. He also nodded to one of the assembly girls, who smiled back at him but that was the only form of communication he had in the company as had been the case for many years because all the employees knew the longest serving deliveryman did not engage in casual chatting, indeed did not engage in any discussions.

At six-twenty-seven, possibly three minutes later than usual, Harry started his loaded van. The unusual delay had been caused by the bakery's large black cat walking casually across the front of Harry's van.

Harry had watched the cat, impressed with its calm control and smooth action, delaying to start the motor until the cat had cleared his view.

On the road making his way to his first café shop/bakery drop off, he fell easily into his habit mode of simply operating the van without the slightest thought, his sub conscious reacting to junctions, traffic lights, crossroads, cyclists, cars on the way early to work, until he drew the van to a stop exactly outside the front door of the 'Cosy Tea Cake and Teashop', as he had been doing for nineteen unbroken years.

As a committed loner, Harry had no interest in holidays, accepting the inconvenience of National and Christmas holidays but perfectly happy to return every day to his rather isolated single bed roomed cottage to spend any free time on his small but perfect garden or with his stamp collection, happy to avoid all but the minimum social interaction with people, as he had managed to do since he was a young boy.

Harry shouldered the bakery tray and as usual the owner was on hand to open the door and once Harry had slid the tray on to the front counter, received the proffered customary mug of tea with a nod.

"Going to be wet later, Harry," advised the owner, who always gave Harry his first weather report of the day as he carried on.

"Looks as if the PM is going to have his work cut out to get any sense from those EU politicians, and I see United are going to lose their Manager,"

Harry sipped his tea and nodded at appropriate points as the news was transmitted to him. Finally, with a nod and with a, "Same time tomorrow," comment, he shouldered the previous day's delivery tray and returned to the van, the shopkeeper happy that he had given the taciturn delivery man the day's news.

On his way to his second delivery stop, his mind wandered for a moment over the possibility that he had not added the tomato feed to his watering can before he had watered the plants. The thought was so disturbing that Harry took out his neatly ironed grey handkerchief and vigorously blew his nose.

The procedure was another of the little tricks that Harry used when he was concerned he might be getting into a state of anxiety by thinking of something in his daily routine that he might have missed doing.

Blowing his nose cleared his mind and in his case caused him to recall he had topped up the bird nuts in the box outside the greenhouse, tied the extended shoots on the gladioli plants and indeed had put two spoons of tomato feed into the watering can before watering each plant.

The disturbing thoughts did not disrupt Harry's driving habits and he arrived exactly at seven-thirty as usual at his second delivery and was as usual greeted by the cake shop proprietor at her open door, where as usual he failed to attend to her tirade about her customers. On this morning it was about a certain lady customer and her wretched children who will finger the cakes before choosing one!

Harry nodded in distant agreement as he deposited the goods and collected yesterday's tray before a, "Same time tomorrow," grunt as he slid past her, still verbally protesting the indignities with which she had to contend, on his way out of the door.

Routine delivery followed routine delivery, following Harry's tidy habitual routings. He did occasionally, when the traffic was light or the traffic signal was red, reflect upon the evening task of sorting the 1850 'penny red' stamps in their year order within a new album he had acquired after several weeks of careful consideration over the size, suitability, durability and cost of the albums on offer.

Returning to the depot following his final delivery, Harry was unexpectedly forced to make a deviation from the main road down a country cut through lane as directed by the Water Board's signs and the 'Closed Road' sign.

Only slightly bothered by the inconvenience, Harry followed the lane for some minutes before he was forced to undertake a rapid stop when a small dog ran across the lane in front of him, causing him to step sharply on the brakes concerned he might have hit the dog. Harry pulled into a layby allowing other vehicles to continue their journey before he climbed out of his van.

Harry found a small terrier pup curled up in a ball in the hedge a pace or two back from his van and to his relief as he reached in through the brambles the shivering pup wagged his tail and allowed Harry to stroke him and carefully lift him out of the hedge, once Harry had decided nothing was broken.

Cars continued to pass at a steady rate forcing Harry to push into the hedge to avoid them and he became fearful for the little chap, and so holding him with one arm inside his company jacket he walked back into the cab to decide what he should do.

Several minutes later Harry was no clearer to a solution but the pup had settled on to the passenger seat in complete confidence, as if he owned it.

There were no houses in the immediate vicinity and so short of any ideas Harry pulled out into the traffic to continue his route to the depot.

Half a mile further down the lane the pup was sitting up and most comfortable when Harry caught sight of a sign 'Waifs and Strays Dog Charity' and he pulled the van over, encouraged by the thought he had found the pup's home

With the pup under his arm, Harry knocked on the house front door which was opened by a small rather care worn lady in an overall with 'Waifs and Strays Dog Charity' insignia on the pocket.

"This," said Harry, "may be one of yours," as he proffered the terrier pup forward.

"Yes," said the lady, without accepting the offered pup. "He escaped when the Vet was here."

"Well," said Harry, "would you like the little fellow back now?"

"Not really," said the lady. "All the litter were put down and the Vet's gone now."

"Put down." Harry was startled and horrified as he pulled the pub back to his chest. "Why? What had they done?"

"Nothing," continued the lady sadly, "but the mother and the pubs were dumped on us and although we found homes for three and the mother, we simply have no money or space in the charity to keep more than the forty dogs and we had no option. Could you keep this little chap, otherwise I'm afraid he will have to go when the Vet visits next?"

Harry positively spluttered as he reeled away from the thought that the pup would be killed.

"But he cannot cost much to keep and this is a charity."

"It's a charity with no money and forty dogs to feed," said the lady. "To be honest I simply do not know how to keep going from one day to the next."

Harry then said the first spontaneous thing he had said in years.

"I'll keep him," and to his own amazement he did not feel even a twinge of the sort of anxiety that normally overcame him whenever he did anything, or said anything out of his normal routine.

The lady looked pleased and relieved.

"Come in a minute," she said beckoning him to follow her. "I have a leaflet which explains what he should eat and helpful notes on getting him settled in."

She led the way into a small neat office, filled with files and dog products.

"Sit down I will make you a cup of tea."

Harry sat obediently with the pup on his lap.

Harry was so disturbed to have moved out of his pedestrian comfort zone, he blurted out a question.

"But why are things so bad for you? You are providing a service to the community."

Had he given himself time to consider the matter he would have recognised this was the longest sentence he had spoken to anyone for several years. Indeed, since the day that a post van had backed into his van.

The lady returned to the room saying, "Here's your tea, do you take sugar? By the way I'm Mary Jones," she continued. "Well we were fine until the lovely lady who raised funds for us in the area died last year and I just cannot look after the dogs, deal with trying to place them and raise money. I am working every hour god gave me now. What's your name?"

She carried on writing in a large ledger.

"Oh, er, Harry Higgins," and without her asking Harry gave his address.

"Well, Harry, you have really cheered me up taking the lovely little chap on, so as you don't live very far away, perhaps you would call and let me know how he gets on? What are you going to call him?"

"Well I hadn't thought, Mary," replied Harry.

And surprised as he realised he had called her by her first name without embarrassment, he went on.

"You see, I was diverted down your lane, just by chance, and there he was in the lane in front of my van. Would you think 'Chance' would be a good name for him?"

Mary clapped her hands, "How appropriate, look he already knows."

'Chance' had stood up on his sturdy little legs on Harry's lap, ears pricked, tail wagging, whether in response to the hand clap or his name was not really clear.

Back at the depot Harry parked the van and with Chance in his arms he walked into the factory where suddenly he was surrounded by smiling bakery workers wanting to see and pat the pup, complimenting Harry on his decision to take on the unwanted dog.

Harry found that all the attention did not throw him into a nervous retreat, as it most certainly would have only earlier that morning.

Indeed with Chance wagging his tail and clearly loving the attention, Harry felt a warm glow of comfort that he had somehow stepped over the protective wall of disciplined routine which he had hidden behind for so many years, thanks to his new four-legged friend.

A week later with Chance in a bright red collar, Harry knocked on the door of the 'Waifs and Strays Dog Charity' which was opened by Mary. She smiled.

"My goodness how well and smart Chance looks. I have told lots of people your story, Harry, and got one or two donations because of it. Now come in both of you."

Sitting down with a cup of tea, Harry said.

"Look I have thought a good deal about our meeting and I was wondering if I could help you raise money for the charity by taking Chance around and telling people our story. I take Chance out with me on my rounds in the mornings and I have seen how the customers respond to him and I thought we might do more for you."

Mary's face was beaming. "What a lovely idea. Thank you so much, Harry. Anyway who are we to decide, look at Chance's tail going, he obviously approves."

Maintaining the Traditions

Andrew (Andy) Osborne walked disconsolately across the school yard. The Victorian fine story buildings full of windows on either side of him seemed to be frowning down as he humped his sports bag higher over his shoulder and slouched his way to the gym. His head was filled with 'this is my last chance' thoughts and the dreadful black cloud of despair swept over him as he went through the high stone entrance with the bold statement 'Achievement brings Success' chiselled into the stone work above him. Inside the sports hall Andy could hear boys laughing and joking before he pushed through the swing doors.

Andy could see above the heads of the boys as his one metre and eighty-six centimetres towered over every other boy in the hall.

Once he was in the hall, Andy looked left and right for his friend Neville (Nev), who was one of the shortest of all the senior boys and with the events about to be announced the only boy Andy felt comfortable to be standing with.

Filled with anxiety and a feeling of impending dread, Andy was surprised by Nev, who arrived behind him and dug him in the ribs.

"What a bloody pain all these top team announcements are," said Nev. "Everyone already knows if he is in the teams or, in our case, not. Why they just don't put a list on the board and leave it at that without putting us through all this b***s*it, I don't know."

"It's all right for you," said Andy, "you haven't got the family name on every Annual Sports Achievement Board since time began, and when I leave this wretched place finally without my name in some team or the other, I will be the first sports failure in our family for a zillion years," and he added, "my father will have me down as an embarrassing failure at the school. At least your family don't expect anything and don't mind."

"Listen up, listen up," Mr Humphrey's loud sonorous voice boomed over the heads of all the boys and an expectant silence descended on the gathered throng.

Flanked by his two Assistant Sports Masters Mr Humphreys, called 'humpy' by the boys very much behind his back said, "Now the school's year teams which will be recorded on the school Sports Achievement Board are, First the Rugby team." He said 'Rugby' with considerable relish. It was the sport he was devoted to in training and competition and the year's success without a single loss to another school, reflected his training skills and the Headmaster and School Board's public congratulations filled him with pride and anticipation the increased bonus he was confidently expecting.

The expected rugby teams names were read out before Mr Humphreys went on to announce the Hockey and Tennis teams, followed in steady order by the Swimming and finally the year Fencing team.

When just for a second Andy wondered if by some miracle his awkward and ungainly style with the 'Epee' might have just got him on the team, but no as expected his name was not announced by Mr Humphreys.

Dispensing to their form rooms, Andy and Nev trudged back across the school yard. "Surely your dad is pleased you got to Uni with straight 'A's," said Nev.

"No, not really, I don't think he cares a bugger. He just wanted our family name on the Sports Achievement Board like my great-grandfather, my grandfather and him. Now I will leave school with nothing, all that tradition crap broken, that's all he seems to care about."

"Well, what about your mum, she can see that you being so tall makes the playing of sports difficult, can't she?"

"Well," replied Andy, "I think she does but she doesn't say much. I suppose she sees my dad is so disappointed about the family name and everything."

Andy was very relieved to find his father out when he got home and he did not have to go through the painful explanation that his name had not appeared in any of the school's teams Annual Achievements lists.

In his bedroom that night, Andy lay on his bed with his head on the pillow in tears, feeling on his own and overcome by the feeling he had let the family and family name down, and that he would carry the shame for ever.

Andy hardly slept that night, wakened by nightmares of being on his own in an alien world, desperately searching for someone to talk to as the people he approached all turned their backs on him.

In the morning the breakfast was conducted in almost total silence, broken only by, "Please pass the marmalade," and, "Another cup of tea?" from his mother.

In school, form time hour with the Master, Mr Fothergill, was spent sorting out each boy's clutter at the end of the academic year. For those like Andy leaving for University, he had to make sure that each student's personal item were accounted for correctly. Mr Fotheringill called Andy to his desk and said, "Andy, would you see the Headmaster's Secretary. She needs someone to help on a job for the school and I told her you had finished all your end of year work and tasks and were ready for the university move. I don't know what she needs help with but it could be the 'last day' event with the parents, governors, etc. See Mrs James in the next period would you? I have told Mr Grey you will be skipping his English Lit. Class and he quite understood."

Mrs James, a statuesque lady of indeterminate years, much fantasized over by junior boys still missing their mothers in the first form, welcomed Andy into her office.

"Ah, Andy, I am so glad you were able to help me. I need someone sensible. Now how are you feeling as you get into your last couple of weeks here at school?"

Andy, who had always liked and trusted Mrs James, was suddenly rather overwhelmed with the despondent thought that he would have to tell his father that his name would not appear on one of this year's sports team lists. Knowing how disappointed his father would be that the unbroken line of sporting excellence by members of the family had come to an end.

"Well actually, Mrs James. I am feeling really down having to explain to my parents that I failed to get into a school team and I tried pretty hard. I'm just not enthusiastic about sports and I feel depressed. Everyone knows how clumsy and uncoordinated I am. Not like my dad or any of the other members of my family."

"Sit down, Andy. Here is a cup of tea and look I have found a couple of chocolate biscuits. Now I know how important sports excellence has been to your family but you are one of our brightest and most sensitive pupils and in the end that is really a great achievement, even if it is not always recognised."

Mrs James continued in her quiet but authoritative way. "Now finish your tea. I want you to cycle round to the clinic where they help the damaged young service personnel in the village, with this letter inviting any of those going through rehabilitation to join our Christmas Carol Concert here at the school. The Headmaster thought it would be nice if one or two of these unfortunate young men with limb damage or psychological damage from the tour of duty in the Middle East were to join us. I am not sure any will come but you never know and I am sure it's worth a try to ask them."

Andy cycled down to the village with the Headmaster's letter safely in his breast coat pocket. He made his way down the tree-lined drive to the imposing country house, now converted into the military clinic and recovery centre for damaged service men.

Andy left his bicycle beside the front porch and pulled the bell pull.

There was a long delay and then Andy heard a strange squeaking sound and the door opened slightly, revealing a tyre and a voice which said, "Could you give the door a bit of a push. I have not quite got the hang of managing my wheelchair yet."

Andy obliged by carefully pushing the door open wider as the wheel retreated into the porch.

"Come in, come in," said a young man in the wheelchair, the stump of his right leg below the knee bandaged and protruding as he swiftly rotated his chair and made off down the long tiled corridor, pumping the driving wheels on the left and right of his seat vigorously with his arms and talking as he did so.

"I'm Jack, only been here from the Afghanistan Bomb Recovery Squad for a month. I'm playing in the handball game in the gym but I got tipped over which is why I got delegated to answer the bell. What's your name?"

Andy quickly replied as Jack continued manoeuvring down the corridor.

"Oh OK, Andy, who do you want to see? Oh, OK it's the CO for you. We will shoot round to his office."

Andy practically had to jog to keep up with Jack who stopped opposite a substantial wooden door with a sign across it 'Major General Gerald Sparrow, Officer Commanding'.

"Knock and go straight in," commanded Jack. "See you later," and he was gone.

Andy knocked and went in where he found a lady in a white medical coat sitting at a desk in front of a computer. She smiled and Andy explained the purpose of his visit.

"Oh yes, your School Secretary called to say someone would deliver the letter." She stood and enquired as to Andy's name before she knocked and entered the inner door. Almost immediately coming out and with another smile she said, "Go in and explain your visit to our CO."

Andy nervously went through the door to find a grey haired, slim gentleman, in a white medical coat advancing towards him with this hand outstretched.

"Welcome, how nice of you to visit. We love to see young men come here to meet our young chaps. I understand you have met Jack. He is one of our latest members here to get used to getting mobile again."

The CO took Andy's arm and led him to two comfortable chairs in the corner of his office.

"Now let me see the letter but then tell me what you think about us being involved with your school event.

Within half an hour, Andy found himself highlighting the good things about his school to the CO who listened carefully, before he said.

"Listen, Andy, you are clearly a bright and able young man and going on to university and no doubt to a great career. Some of my chaps have to start over again when they thought they had made a career choice, through no fault of their own. If you can spare half an hour I will take you down to meet one or two of the men playing basketball. I know they would be interested to meet you."

Andy found himself watching twelve twirling wheelchairs as the basketball was flipped, thrown and carried into a net scoring position on the court. He found himself righting a wheelchair, using the lifting bar as pointed out by the Drill

Sergeant Instructor, benefitting from his height to complete the lift in one easy action.

Andy was really enjoying the activity and found himself getting several servicemen upright and then being introduced by Jack to the members of both squads. He was so involved he did not notice the CO had quietly returned to his office.

As Andy left to find his bicycle, the CO's Secretary found him and said.

"The CO wonders if you could pop in to see the boys for an hour tomorrow to explain to the chaps how you got your University place."

Andy visited every day, thoroughly enjoying the camaraderie and being involved in the life of the recovery unit in various ways, from helping out with the English tutorials to socialising with the young men, some emotionally damaged, who needed to talk to someone used to the clubs and social events they knew they would have to engage with in the world to which they would soon be returning.

On the afternoon of the last day of term and for Andy the last day at his school, the hall was packed with boys and their parents, the School Board and the Headmaster were on the stage, with the school choir behind them.

To the surprise of most a section at the front of the hall was cordoned off.

A minute before the formal start the double doors at the rear of the hall opened fully and the Major General in full uniform entered with several officers, followed by twenty soldiers in uniform on crutches, or in wheelchairs, who all took their place in the front of the school assembly.

The Headmaster graciously and fully welcomed his new arrivals before the Carol Service was vigorously engaged in by everyone, including the servicemen.

At the end of the Carol Service the Headmaster spoke of the school year, referring to high points and as was customary, referring to the outstanding sportsmen to go on to the 'Victor Ludorum' Board of Achievement.

Andy sank into his jacket, highly sensitive to his family name not being on any of the year's teams, although his mother gave his arm a comforting squeeze.

"And finally," said the Headmaster, "the Board have decided to issue each year a new medal for Achievement to a boy who has successfully promoted the standards and quality of our school and this first Medal for Excellence goes to Andrew Osborne — please come forward Andrew."

'Lord of All He Surveys'

The day that Reginald Walter Stone took up his role as Chief Executive Officer of Techno-Connect will be long remembered by those that survived his regime.

The recently retired CEO had enjoyed an easy relationship with his staff and his avuncular style encouraged the staff to support his actions, even to cover for events when some of his strategic decisions were shown to lack financial return for the effort. In his last few years in charge, decisions over marketing strategy did nothing to help the company's performance in an ever more competitive electrical interconnecting component manufacturing market.

The company had evolved from a defence contractor in WW2 into a comfortable, steady growth, steady profit, performer where the company's team had a reputation for professional integrity and a willingness to help their customers to keep their electrical motors and electronic equipment going, often when the components were shocked and shaken in hot or cold conditions year in, year out.

The long established board of directors who regularly picked up their fees, expenses and dividends without fuss or bother, occasionally wondered over their post board meeting dinner drinks whether a new young CEO might not 'zip up' the company's performance, but as the small, close knit, board of directors were in the same age group as the CEO and had grown comfortable over many years, they slid back into their after dinner seats and debated rather more on the weakness in the English cricket team than the company.

It was only when the CEO's wife put her foot firmly down and insisted he retire to the garden, bowls club and the grandchildren precisely on his sixty-fifth birthday that the Chairman and the Board woke up, and short of other ideas an expensive London recruitment agency was hired.

The selection was made and Reg Stone swept through the front door to take up his role as the company's leader.

With boundless self-confidence Reg Stone dazzled the Board into silence as he amplified, emphasised and embellished his CV details under the banner of bringing 'positive international growth' to the company, all thanks to his experience as a Senior Manager of a competitor when, according to him, his experience and skills in breaking into the US market would, without any doubt, galvanise Techno-Connect into becoming the UK's leading specialist connector manufacturers.

The Chairman and the Board listened and nodded sagely hoping that whatever the changing strategies being threatened they would not be too disruptive to their own comfortable benefits from the company. Each, however privately, having a queasy feeling privately that they had lost the control they had always enjoyed.

Reg Stone's first morning priority was to sit and survey the scene from his CEO chair. Holding up the bone china coffee cup brought in by the rather elderly secretary, a feeling of considerable self-satisfaction swept over him. Here he was against all the odds sitting here, the king of all he surveyed. Where were directors in his old company now, always pointing the finger at his lack of taste, always criticising in everything in which he was involved? *Now*, thought Reg Stone, *they must be reflecting on how wrong they were to misjudge his ability*.

Reg Stone spoke kindly to his Secretary and asked her to call in the young, recently recruited, HR Manager.

Reg Stone had done his homework before he had arrived, beginning with the people in 'his team'. Confident that if he selected and sorted them quickly

deciding on those most likely to be 'loyal' to his directions, he would very soon control the whole company and then be able to implement his strategy to bring it up to performance speed and in a direction he felt appropriate to generate serious commission for himself and to ensure his independence from any interference from the decrepit Board and the ossified old Chairman.

Reg Stone set about his task that first day with some vigour and within the week he had identified his top tier team and made quite clear to them individually that their survival in the company and their remuneration depended upon their following his every direction in unquestioning support.

Reg Stone was pleased to find that his passion in life, Formula 1 car racing, had been seen as a market for the new company which the company was developing and had made some minor sales, led by the recently engaged Sales Manager, Terry.

Looking for a new leadership role to impress the board and the company, Reg Stone encouraged Terry to promote the potential for the multi-pin aircraft designed connectors in the race car market.

And within a month Reg Stone had elevated the young manager's responsibilities, giving him the authority to get first priority for engineering developments to suit Formula 1 race car teams' connector interest with the promise that developing this aspect of the business was his route to early directorship.

Within no time, Reg Stone's enthusiastic drive meant a range of modified interconnecting devices were being offered to Formula 1 teams in the UK and abroad, from McLaren to

Ferrari, and with young Terry working hard in the field, the concept was quickly successful.

Indeed, thanks to hard driving sales and luck in hitting the pre-season preparation time for the Formula 1 teams, the majority of the Formula 1 cars on the Silverstone grid for the start of the year's first race were revving up their engines, thanks to the new Techno-connect multi-pin light weight connectors.

The season went from strength to strength as Formula 1 car racing went around the world on the F1 circuits demonstrating and promoting the Techno-connect product. Attracting increased business which required Reg Stone and his support management to swiftly reschedule the company's manufacturing and assembly facilities and refocus his design and engineering team towards the highly profitable Formula 1 product range, and as a result dumping their traditional products.

Inevitably, as Reg Stone saw it, there were some redundancies in the workforce even dismissals from the longer serving workforce who could not keep up with the speed of change, which all rather tended to increase the company's profit margins, as Reg Stone was pleased to hear the company's accountant say.

Reg Stone revelled in his growing notoriety as a 'strong man', and an incisive leader. He also indulged himself in the glow of the spotlight from the motoring press and the Formula 1 car manufacturers and their sponsors now anxious to have his opinions on a range of front edge technologies for these leaders of Formula 1 race car motor technology.

Reginald Stone, as he liked to be addressed now, radically changed the company's manufacturing processes to focus upon the multi-pin connectors exclusively for race cars, abruptly terminating long serving customer contracts for the company's traditional ranges.

Despite complaints and concerns the Board kept quiet as the profits rocketed and under Reginald's brisk meetings where his 'golden future strategy' was emphasised with finger strumming enthusiasm to the Directors as the race season progressed.

Reginald Stone's ego was puffed up at every turn and when he was invited to join a BBC Television panel discussing the future of Formula 1 racing for the benefit of the UK's standing in the advanced technology world, he knew he had 'arrived'.

As he explained to his wife before the programme, over his second bottle of wine, the importance of his leadership and inspirational strategic decisions would soon result in him taking over the chairmanship of the board and becoming a significant shareholder in the group as he did so. His wife's only response was to indicate her concern over his increased alcohol intake and the dangers of his heightened blood pressure his doctor had warned him about.

At dinner that night he had arranged with one or two of his previous company's cronies and their wives, he luxuriated in the stream of compliments about his television success, although one of the wives did quite unnecessarily, he thought, refer to his expanded waste line since she had last seen him.

On their way home Reginald's wife did say, again rather unnecessarily, he thought, "You know, Jane is quite right. You have put on a bit of weight and it cannot be good for you, especially as you are so busy and now in the media view."

"Oh she was just being bitchy because John is thin as a pin and is probably nagged all the time. I don't worry work wise, my team are all totally committed to my success programme. I can ease back a bit as next year is going to be really big and I will buy that holiday flat in Tenerife you are always going on about."

The Formula 1 season ended and the company Board gave Reg Stone a celebratory dinner in a prestigious hotel, giving him a silver salver marked 'Reginald Stone – A Racing Star' to please him.

The Chairman also handed him an envelope with a considerable bonus cheque in it with nods of approval saying.

"Reginald, we are men of our word, when you produce results as you have we will always directly reflect this in your remuneration and with the results going as well as they are, this time next year we will be talking shareholding."

At the end of the Formula 1 season and in the quiet period before the preparations and engineering upgrades for the next season, Reginald called his team to prepare their strategy.

Terry, the Sales Manager, had the floor as the man most closely involved with the industry and to everyone's surprise he indicated a radical change might be needed to provide contacts to join the new 'glass fibre' cables within the connectors as this form of high speed data transfer was, he felt, likely to have its place and weight saving in the Formula 1 cars.

Reginald, surprised and dismayed, was quick to stamp out these thoughts, emphasizing the importance of building on their core experience in interconnecting technology for the next year. As he explained later to Terry who had not been happy by the public 'put down' from Reginald to his carefully considered strategic approach for the new season.

"These little technology ideas are always going to pop up and then disappear and all they do is get people to lose focus on our core job. Now off you go, get out to our customers and trust me to keep us strategically on track."

A week later Terry came into Reginald Stone's office to tender his resignation to the considerable annoyance of Reginald who said, "Well if all my help and guidance means so little to you, you can forget a month's notice, clear your desk and go off to our competitor and much good it will do you, but don't think you can knock on my door for your old job half way through the season."

A month into the preparation period for all the Formula 1 teams it was clear to everyone in the company that things were going dramatically wrong.

The new hybrid electrical/optical connectors supplied by the company's competitor and the new 'home' of Terry, the Sales Director, were dominating the orders from the Formula 1 car manufacturers.

Techno-connect, led by a more and more desperate Reginald, found themselves virtually only supplying traditional connectors where maintenance equipment needed to be replaced.

Worst still under his emphatic leadership, all the older traditional connector assembly lines and tools had been discarded and so the company could no longer respond to enquiries from their old customers for their core business products.

Handing in her notice the bright young Accountant announced to Reginald that the company had gone into the red in last month's trading.

Reginald retreated to his office and the whisky bottle and three days later whilst he was sitting disconsolately slumped in his new chrome and leather seat, the Chairman and the Board arrived, unannounced.

"Well, Reg you have got the company into a fine mess," was the Chairman's opening shot.

"We have no option but to give you a month's notice for termination of your contract with us. You will recall you insisted upon a performance-measured contract that required the company to be continuously very profitable, and clearly it is not. I have called your wife who is on her way, and collected the company's Jaguar key from your secretary."

And with this and much nodding of heads and tutting from the Board, they all swept out of the office.

Half an hour later, Reg's wife came into the office to find him being sick in his recently installed washroom.

"There, there, Reg," she said sharply, "wipe your face and blow your nose, things could be worse. Now you will be able to spend time in the garden. I am sure that will help you lose some weight and thank goodness you had not got round to signing for that flat in Tenerife. You know you can now spend more time collecting pictures of Formula 1 drivers and cars for your album. I know you will love to do that, so now come along, put on your scarf, its cold outside and I will drive you home."

A Voice from the Grave

"We are gathered here today in St Cuthbert's to celebrate a great and generous man. Charles Everett, CBE whose passing has left a gap in our community, his corporation and family.

I know many of you would like to speak on his behalf and I hope you will forgive me for calling but a few to represent the many groups and companies to whom he gave his support so whole-heartedly.

For my part at St Cuthbert's, Charles' support as a member of our congregation and a Church Warden despite his business responsibilities and his need to travel round the world will be much missed."

Standing in his pulpit the Reverend Eldridge glanced obviously at his watch, a signal he hoped to those he was going to call to speak to keep their comments short and to the point, as he had.

"Now may I invite Mr Grant, Charles' lawyer from the distinguished Solicitors Grant Simmons?"

Reverend Eldridge felt that the small promotion referring to 'distinguished' would not go amiss amongst the large local audience, particularly as he knew he would need legal advice to stop the Adventure Ramblers Association using the St Cuthbert's entrance to make their way up to the Downs every weekend!

Vincent Grant rose from the front row of the pews, immaculate in a 'slim fit' dark blue suit, to step up into the pulpit where he paused to stretch his arms slightly to ensure his perfect white cuffs and his gold Rolex showed. Satisfied he had the audience's attention he announced.

"I had the privilege of helping Charles Everett as he built his business empire and in his wide range of other interests over twenty-five years."

Vincent Grant continued to laud Charles Everett for a few more minutes before he said.

"Charles left me instructions to say that beyond the arrangements under his Will, he intends to make bequests to several local organisations in which he had interested himself over the years and Grant Simmons will be contacting these organisations in due course."

The Reverend Eldridge frowned severely over his spectacles at the murmur of discussion that Vincent Grant's final comments had created. He then nodded to indicate to the first of the selected speakers they should step up to the pulpit.

Several speakers followed each other, all eulogising Charles Everett's influence and support with various levels of presentational competence, taking various styles from the 'homely' through the 'tear jerk emotional' and even the 'this was a funny one' remembrances until the Reverend Eldridge drew a close to the 'celebrations' by indicating that care would be needed getting away from the church car park and in case it had not been noticed, the church maintenance fund box was on the left of the door as they departed.

The Reverend Eldridge was very conscious as people drifted out of the church that he was speaking that afternoon to the members of the Women's Institute, not a group he would wish to disappoint by being late.

A few days after the 'celebration' St Cuthbert's several local organisations received a letter of instruction from the late Charles Everett via his solicitor, Vincent Grant.

The letter indicated that if they were interested in benefitting from Mr Everett's estate, they needed to put down on 'one piece of paper' the key points of their intentions to build their business or their activity over the next three years.

Their ideas would then be considered by an independent business consultant before the beneficiaries could be advised.

As the letter explained, Mr Everett's interest and long term support had covered local businesses, including a charity, and his son's musical business, explaining this was why the request was made in these terms.

The solicitor's letter caused considerable discussion and some controversy within the organisations that Charles Everett had taken an interest in over the years.

The Chairman's meeting at the golf club where Charles had played, conducted a very heated meeting when he accused the Secretary of not 'following-up' his demand for a sizeable donation from Charles Everett for the club house extension 'while he was still alive'.

The committee all knew the Chairman had invited a minor Royal to open the extension, confident that Charles would provide the building fund and he would now see himself being embarrassed.

The garden centre where Charles had provided the funds for a tropical plant greenhouse considered the request for a possible donation to install a humidifier exactly as if Charles had been sitting with them.

Charles' one and only son, Richard, known as 'Ricky' in the music promotion business, a not very successful 'chip off the business block', was bemoaning the regular loss of financial support he had received from his father which had kept the bank off his bank despite the trading losses, his thoughts on what to put in his 'single request sheet' not being helped by the bottle of whisky with which he had fortified himself.

At the 'New Start' Charity for single mothers, many with personal or partner problems, providing accommodation, counselling and a range of supports, Jenny Stirling was recalling with heartache how valuable Charles' financial support had been to get them going and now she believed they could now stand on their own feet, even if they could not extend their services.

The day for the single sheet submissions to be considered duly arrived and Vincent Grant welcomed all the groups before introducing, "Dr Stephen Bailey, a highly experienced business consultant who we have engaged at Charles Everett's request to consider your three year strategic objectives."

Vincent Grant continued, "Before I can say anymore, I am instructed by Mr Everett to play a tape of him explaining his intentions."

Vincent Grant leaned forward and pushed a button on the tape player on his desk. Four speakers in the room projected Charles Everett's voice as clearly and precisely as if he was in the room with them.

"Friends, I have come to realise, rather too late, that I have done you all a disservice in supporting you year on year with gifts of money, believing this would help your organisations.

I now realise I was propping up things for you without encouraging you to manage your own organisations in a planned way. You have now prepared your 'Business Plan'.

The fact that this tape is being played to you means that my anticipations about your determination to think out a three year plan were right and therefore my final offer of support can be passed to you by Vincent, my lawyer, and I wish you all well in your endeavours."

In the silence that followed Vincent cleared his throat.

"Charles Everett's instructions to me are that providing you sign up to an agreement, Dr Stephen Bailey will work over the next three years with each group to help you realize your Business Plans.

In addition money has been put aside to build fifty residential units for single disadvantaged women with children, managed by the 'New Start' Charity. This programme to be overseen by Dr Bailey.

And finally my son, Richard Everett, will receive financial support to maintain his music business, overseen by Dr Bailey, providing he agrees to give twenty hours of his time every month to the 'New Start' Charity to work with the disadvantaged ladies and their families as instructed by Jenny Stirling in the hope that he will come to realise that a practical and productive life cannot be achieved by looking at life through the bottom of a whisky glass."

Enjoying the Job

"Kevin, do you have a minute?"

Kevin, head down at his desk staring into his computer whilst trying to finish a tuna mayonnaise sandwich, was immediately conscious that his work area was an over cluttered battle field which might, he reasoned anxiously, be giving rise to the beckoning finger.

Hastily gulping down the last of his sandwich and wiping his mouth with the back of his hand, Kevin kicked back his chair and followed the retreating back of the Department Manager who was shuffling between crowded computer desks in order to get back into his own office.

"Sit down Kevin," said AJ to Kevin who was hovering anxiously at the door. "Now you have been with us," and he glanced at the screen in front of him, "nearly three months this summer. I have been talking about your contribution to our owner, Giles, as you are one of the 'Standout Students' of this summer's intake."

AJ paused and eyed Kevin who was sitting on the edge of his seat.

"Your work and creative thinking on the software development packages you have been given to think about has been 'top drawer' and," AJ continued, "to cut to the chase, Giles would like to have a personal chat with you tomorrow before you leave us."

Kevin twisted awkwardly on his chair, pleased and anxious at the same time.

AJ saw his confusion and said, "Listen Kev, you really have a talent for our kind of creative work and that's a rare thing. Now I know you are planning to go on to Uni to get a computer programming degree, and that's the conventional way for you to take the first step in your career, but there are other ways of getting on and I know Giles wants to share some thoughts with you tomorrow."

That evening he finished his mid-week training session on the recreation ground with the St Ethelred's FC training squad and was told by the Manager, Josh, that he was in the coming Saturday's home game, retaining his half back place, before Josh's team talk over emphasising, as he always did, the difficulties the team would be facing as if St Ethelred's amateur third division side were taking on Arsenal on the recreation ground.

When he arrived home Kevin explained to his dad the content of his unexpected discussion with AJ, his computer software company's Office Manager.

In the comfortable relationship Kevin had with his dad, he felt no need to hold back his thoughts, despite the family's long-term commitment for him to go to University, with all the costs this would require of the family and with Kevin's sixteen-year-old brother shaping to follow the same route two years later on.

"You see, Dad, AJ says I am a 'natural', whatever that means, at seeing creative software development opportunities and maybe the owner, Giles, is thinking he might give me a job when I finish Uni. You never know he might even offer me a way of paying some of my fees if I would accept going into 'Zipby' when I finish the degree. I would, and that would help when Jimmy leaves school for Uni, wouldn't it?"

"Well it certainly might, son, but your mum and me just want what is best for you and your future and you know we have put the money by for your fees for the first two years and the way our garden equipment repair service is going, we should be able to finance your third year. Of course, you getting a part-time job at Uni and the good money you have put by from working at Zipby I should think will give you enough funds to get the odd beer and do your social thing, and cover the travel costs back and forth and, as your mum always says, your laundry and heaven knows how much credit you have in that, what is it? Hero Story computer games where you have all those game credits you can sell for cash next month when you're eighteen!

"No, I don't want to know how much," Kevin's dad went on, holding up his hand. "Your mother would have a fit if she knew. You know she doesn't approve of you 'gambling' as she calls it on the computer and incidentally she is right. You do spend a great deal of time now in front of the screen. I wonder that nice girlfriend of yours has any time for you when you can hardly tear yourself away on a Saturday night."

Taking his 'Anytime Rest' break at ten in the luxurious Zipby canteen, Kevin had hardly time to consume his jam and cream filled donut or down his latte coffee from the extensive 'Help Yourself' stainless steel display shelves all offering a wide range of 'freebie' food perks for all the employees when his mobile beeped a *'pop into my office when you can'* signal from Giles, an instruction everyone knew had to be responded to immediately.

The sumptuously appointed office enveloped Kevin as he shuffled anxiously behind Giles' elegantly tailored Secretary, whose 'welcome everyone' dazzling show of teeth together with the fact that she stood several inches taller than Kevin made him feel even more uncomfortable as he looked up to smile back at her.

"Hi, great to see you, Kev," said Giles.

Giles put a Gucci covered arm displaying his heavy gold bracelet Rolex watch over Kevin's shoulder as he guided him to a white leather sofa in the corner of the office, dominated by a highly coloured, totally indecipherable, limited edition print in an elegant chrome frame.

"Tea, coffee, juice, whatever, you call the shot and Petronella will get it for you. Actually," he said to Kevin in an overly theatrical way, "she's actually called Jane but you know, the new Monica, makes the clients more comfortable… you know, fitting our image."

Kevin nodded, without saying anything.

"Let me explain why I am grateful you and I are having this private chat before you leave us."

"You are the best short term student we have ever had on board and this is not me just saying it. I have the report from the management team who say you have a natural creative technical talent, and so, although I know you are planning to go off to do a degree at Uni I would like you to consider, with your family, an offer to start work here at Zipby. The offer is pretty comprehensive to include a share owner aspect that I am sure you will want to talk over with your parents, even though as a very talented eighteen year old, I guess you will make your own decision. So I have had it all typed up."

And with this Giles took the bulky envelope from the white marble-topped coffee table in front of them, and thrust it into Kevin's hand.

"Well there we are, call me when you have given the matter thought, any time, day or night. We don't sleep here, much too busy growing."

Standing in his fashionably designed jeans, Giles swept his arm expansively over his office.

"This office, this whole Zipby organisation, the family friendly hundred and ten people, this is a company that did not exist as a group only three years ago. Imagine Kev where we, and perhaps you, will be three years from now."

Over supper that evening Kevin shared the contents of the envelope while his dad and brother looked on. His mother cleared up the plates and went off to the kitchen to load up the dishwasher having declared. "I wouldn't understand all that stuff. Kevin you and your dad will have to decide what to do. The only thing I can say is you will have to make your mind up quickly because if you don't take up your Uni accommodation, we will want to get the deposit back and cancel that Education Fund application for your course fees."

This said, she swept into the kitchen and shut the door, firmly.

An hour later with the papers spread over the table Kevin's dad said.

"There's no doubting they really want you, that starting salary is nearly what I can earn in our garden machinery maintenance business if everything goes well in the year and from what this letter says the group share bonus could be significant at the end of the year. Then there is the Employee Share thing. We will have to talk to your uncle, he understands this sort of scheme but it looks to me as the longer you stay the more shares you get given and if, well when, the company goes public or is sold, you get the cash. Well I'm sure you will have to pay tax but it still sounds like a 'something for nothing' scheme."

Kevin's brother chimed in. "And all those perks, free grub, and when I'm eighteen you could get me a job."

The match went well on Saturday and St Ethelred had triumphed with a late goal over their local nearest rivals in the league. Celebrations were called for.

Despite this Kevin was worried as he gelled and combed his hair in a style which he knew Liz liked. Although he was not much given to bothering about what he wore, he put on slacks and a shirt which he knew Liz would approve of before he caught the bus into the centre of the town and sauntered up to the club entrance to get his new eighteen plus card scrutinized by the security guard.

Inside, with a wave at mates, he was joined by Liz his girlfriend of more than two years.

During the whole process of getting ready and travelling to the club Kevin had been running through the Zipby offer in his mind, bothered by its unexpected arrival and the scale of the offer which rather frightened him and attracted him at the same time.

In what was a relatively quiet corner of the club with a couple of overpriced low alcohol drinks that for once Kevin insisted on buying, he explained to Liz the drama of his meeting with Zipby's owner and summarised the offer without exaggerating the details.

Liz, who worked in an accountant's office, did not do a 'shocked, amazed' response to the news. She actually said, "I have heard of start-up company's offering big money and shares and things to get the best technical guys they can, and you have always been super good at developing your computer software, and they know you actually built your computer from parts so you can always adjust it to take on the latest developments."

"I dunno, they might do, I can't remember if I ever talked about it. Anyway what do you think, you know I'm all set up to go to Uni and now I am, like, confused what I should do."

Liz looked at him sympathetically.

"Well I guess you will just have to make the decision. I know when I got the job at Blaydons and got my first cheque, it changed a hell of a lot. You know I felt independent. The money made a big difference and I was respected at work, no longer treated like a school kid."

The following morning Kevin told his mum and dad he had decided to take the job.

Papers signed and the Uni advised, two weeks later Kevin found himself with Giles' designer shirt arm around his shoulder in front of a brand new desk and computer set, facing the crowded office as Giles announced, "A new star, Kev, has joined the company to help us on to growth and success." This prompted loud cheers and claps as a large birthday style cake was paraded in by the company chef and everyone gathered around Kevin, shaking his hand and slapping him on the back.

The excitement of his first month and splashing out on a restaurant dinner of celebration for his dad, mum, brother and Liz, getting new designer gear and buying a trendy jacket for Liz was slightly offset by having to work on training nights for the St Ethelred team.

By the end of the second month with a deposit paid for a second hand hatchback, red with black leather interior and his driving test coming up, Kevin was inclined to go to bed well pleased, if well tired.

The months passed and winter turned to spring, Kevin got over being dropped by Josh because as he said, "As long as you cannot get to training I have to pick someone that the team can rely on in the match."

Kevin was upset for some time and missed the training and the camaraderie and explained so to Liz as he drove her in his new motor to the out of town sports centre and club that a colleague had suggested he join as it was open twenty-four-seven, and several of his new colleagues often popped in for a swim and breakfast after an 'all night' work session at Zipby.

Enjoying the work as much as he did, he could not help noticing that Liz was much cooler towards him than before and although he reasoned this was down to having to stand her up on several dates and missing her birthday party, even though he had arranged for a huge bouquet of expensive flowers as an apology for his absence.

Perhaps it was the final Saturday night trip with Liz to the club when she had held his hand as she explained that she was so sorry but because he was so successful and busy she honestly felt Zipby was running his life now and she had her own life to think about, and was determined to do some travelling they had talked about before she settled own, and clearly Kevin would not be able to commit to trips to India,

Malaysia and far places she was determined to experience as soon as she could.

Kevin shamefacedly remembered how often they had talked and planned about these trips during his holiday breaks from Uni, now that matters had been wiped from his 'wish list'. Liz had said she would not do anything behind Kevin's back so she was finishing their relationship that night while they were still friends.

Somehow this event, painful as it was, seemed to be fitting in as part of his new lifestyle governed by the 'Zipby always comes first in all things' culture.

The stress and strain of the twenty-four-seven business and the pressure all the company operators were constantly under caused much discussion about break ups of partnerships and marriages, discussions which were often greeted by fellow team members with comments such as, "Hey, you're young, independent and wealthy, settle down later," variety.

The Zipby team continued to grow week in, week out, as software development programmes followed contract after contract.

Office announcement cheering, razzmatazz and glasses of champagne were fitted in with frequent company masseuse sessions on Kevin's shoulders at the work place, fifteen minute sessions on the mat with the company's Pilate instructor to loosen his 'muscles and the mind' at least three times a week.

Back at home Kevin had been bothered, but somehow not surprised, when his dad and mum were up and sitting round the kitchen table in their dressing gowns one evening close to midnight when he arrived wearily in from Zipby, having eaten a 'take away freebie' provided by the company, and apologised to his parents for the supper, now dried up, that his mother had prepared for seven o'clock.

His Dad said gently, realising how tired he looked.

"Perhaps now is the time for you to think about renting a flat near the office to spare yourself the risky drive when you're tired?"

Painful as the discussion was for the family, common sense guided the decision.

Kevin moved to his own place and some months later Giles called an office 'All Together' meeting with all one hundred and fifty crammed on one floor, sitting uncomfortably on computer stations, spare seats or standing.

Giles, supported by several out of company 'suits', who could have doubled for a mafia crew in a TV film, did the 'more exciting news' arm waving intro before explaining the 'suits' represented new investors who had 'put big bucks' into the company to accelerate the expansion into bigger premises to accommodate the company's 'explosive' growth and the rush to 'go public'.

"Of course," said Giles, "we have had to make changes to the company's shareholdings and naturally the new shareholders have been given preferential shares for their considerable investment which does mean a slight diminution on the value of your 'Employee' shareholdings."

Several days after the 'Exciting News' announcement, during canteen discussions over the changes, Kevin found the paper value of his company shares were now less than half of their original value.

It was this superimposed change to his value to Zipby that caused Kevin to start to revaluate his role and advantages in the start-up company and in his flat relaxing when he arrived back from work, playing on his favourite game where his carefully built-up Avatar character normally battled out with other players, righting wrongs for the weak and under privileged, he found himself in his game situation in 'real time' and all Zipby's carefully structured 'You are a star' hype was just a clever con trick to get young easily persuaded computer enthusiasts into a business start-up where the principals would increase their investment value as quickly as possible on a build-up to go public strategy, which would then leave the majority of the employees high salaries, or not, exposed to the vagaries of the open market and the new owners looking for a better return for their investment.

Kevin began to face up to how little job satisfaction he was getting and how little appreciated he really was, caught in Zipby's 'golden handcuffs' and how isolated from the real world he cared about they had made him.

Looking afresh at himself he also realised that the months he had committed to Zipby culture and his changed lifestyle, the year would not be wasted provided he 'bit the bullet' and took positive action looking to his own future.

On the same day Kevin went and explained matters to his mum and dad.

"I made a mistake in not going to Uni. I was blinded by the new lifestyle and by money but now the experience has shown me I have to do a job where I am valued and that I love doing."

Dad said in response, "Listen Kevin, your mum and brother and I have been really worried about you. We could see you were not happy and getting isolated from all the things you really care about whilst working at Zipby.

"Why don't you come and work in our little business helping me? We are really busy with the machines and perhaps you could also computerise all our records and get our customer service systems in place. I can pay the going rate and from what you were saying you have built up a healthy bank balance, and letting the flat go will all help. It will get you back into the real world and you can make some long term plans then."

After the abrupt 'do you realise what you are giving up' interview with the Personnel Manager, Kevin walked out of the front door of Zipby's palatial foyer without a backward look or a single comment from his Managers, let alone the owner, Giles.

Within a month of his leaving Zipby Kevin had re-established himself in the football squad without as yet getting into the team. He had been able to explain for the hundredth time, without embarrassment, all the perks and big salary did not compensate for an enjoyable nine to five role and time to do things one wanted.

It was true that his couple of attempts to get a date with Liz had come to nought but Kevin felt that if he persisted there might be a chance.

In the garden machinery repair business his computerisation of the customer records was bearing fruit and his dad was delighted with the sudden upturn in business.

Much more relaxed, Kevin began to think about his own future. Should he reapply for Uni next year? He realised the experience in the start-up company, harsh as it was, had given him a taste for business and the reward potential.

Doodling on his computer Kevin began to think the garden machinery experience he now had might offer him a new opportunity and a link for the small domestic gardener looking to their short term needs to cut, prune, lop, turn, excavate, seed, turf and build in environmentally suitable wood, metal, stone and plastic, became a target for him.

With his dad's and brother's support he gathered the support of suppliers prepared to sign-up to 'Gard Find', to assist 'Busy people to rent the right tools for their garden – as and when they needed them.'

A month later and Kevin was shaking hands with a young computer graduate to take on as his first employee.

Smiling as he said, "Look, I only pay the going rate and there really are no perks in the job but if we make the company grow and you enjoy the work, you and I will share a bonus with my dad and brother, and anyone else I take on, at the end of the year, and however well this start-up does, that's the way it's always going to be."

Replicating History

Joseph pulled out the envelope from his writing desk drawer. Tipping the photographs large and small on to his blotter, caught up as he had been many times by the way the faded sandy prints still clear pictures mixed with the sharper black and white shots, transported him back to when his grandfather had sat at the same desk, on the very seat, while he remembered sitting on the stool, now supporting the waste paper basket, listening whilst his grandfather told him stories, showing him photos to illustrate a place, or time in his grandfather's life before the Second World War and on into the nineteen fifties and sixties when he left the Royal Air Force and had to find a job. Not easy when many thousands were doing the same.

Joseph remembered his much loved Grandfather saying, "Now Joseph, remember even if you find yourself doing a not very interesting job to keep your family fed and warm, as I did after the War having to work in the bank as a clerk was really boring, even though your grandmother and I, "bless her soul," knew I needed to stick it out, boring as it was to be able to bring your mother and aunt up in the right way."

Always at this point my grandfather would slide out the several black and white shots of the figurative models he felt were his best-sculptured pieces.

Joseph laid the ten small photos in a row on the purple blotting paper, pushing the remaining photos to one side.

Cheetahs, a lion with a cub, a running wolf, how his grandfather had loved wild animals and how often had he said, "I would love to have visited the game reserves in South Africa to see for myself animals in the wild, not just work from pictures in magazines."

Joseph looked at the photo of the turning and twisting lioness thinking, as he always did, how lucky he was to have the actual model in his bedroom and,

with the same thought, how sad it was his mother had given the rest of his animal models away when his grandfather had died, despite his tears and pleading as she explained, "Look, Joseph we simply cannot fit all of your grandad's bits and pieces into our house, there isn't room, and lots of his friends would like a memento of him and you do have his best model. You know that because he told you and that one is just the right size for your bedside table and as you know he won that national sculptural prize with that casting and he was very proud of that."

Once again Joseph could hear his grandfather's voice telling him that art could be an outlet in your life that let you survive a boring working job.

"Well," thought Joseph, "I sure have a boring job now."

He sat back in the chair holding the photo of his lioness twirling around to catch something. How many times had he laid in bed imagining what the lioness was trying to catch, up on one powerful leg as it twirled its body about? Could she help now?

He was sunk in dismal thoughts about the job's future. Moved off the Sales Desk where at least he could communicate face to face with customers every day, into the back office to take over the job of ordering supplies for the store, a job dominated by the computer screen on his desk in front of him all day long.

"Because," said Mr Simons, the Store Manager, "you know more about our product range than anyone else on the desks. You are a calm, steady man, who doesn't get flustered or excited and I am sure with a bit more money your wife will be pleased with your promotion."

"Never gets flustered or excited, if only he knew how suppressed I am. A thirty-five year old already on the shelf trudging towards retirement," thought Joseph.

Sliding the photos back into the envelope, Joseph opened the drawer to put them away before he noticed one black and white photo left on the blotting pad. He looked at the picture, not of his grandfather's animal models but of the figured ceramic award plate which his grandfather was holding in front of him, rather proudly, about the size of a large dinner plate, various animals around the edge with a rectangular plate at the centre with his grandfather, Frederick Thomson 1960, in raised letters in the middle.

As he had thought one hundred times before, "What a shame the ceramic relief plate was broken when they were clearing out his grandfather's flat, what a shame no one thought to try to put the broken bits together."

At two o'clock in the morning Ann, Joseph's wife, found him sitting at his desk with the same photo in his hand.

"What is wrong, darling, are you ill?"

"No, but I cannot sleep. Grandpa has sent me a message, I'm sure. You know I'm starting that new job on Monday and I am going to try to mend my grandad's award plate. I know I don't have any of his artistic modelling skills but I have got to give it a go. I am sure he knew I would need his support one day and the 'one day' is Monday."

Joseph was well prepared for what was to come on Monday and quickly sorted out a list of priority actions to chase supplies for items he knew were needed at the front desk.

By tea break he recognised that Mr Simons' decision to promote him into the back room had some value and by his lunch break he had some time to think out how he was going to see through his grandfather's project. Thinking as he did, so that his grandpa was in some way 'overseeing the task'.

The night before going through the file of papers his grandfather had left, he found an old catalogue of moulding materials and tools in the name of a London firm, Tiranti, and during his lunch break Joseph phoned the number.

He explained to the company's telephonist that he was anxious to start to sculpture but had no experience or knowledge on the best materials with which to start.

The lady on the phone explained they often received similar calls and there was a lady in Sales who she felt sure could help him.

Sure enough Beth, the lady he was put through to, saved any embarrassment by listing out options and alternatives which depended on his first 'project' and her suggestions, once he had explained his intended effort to replicate a Relief Plate, was to try to do so.

"Using a white wax because it does not dry out and you can keep adjusting the sculpture for days or weeks until you are happy with it and do the work on a large cake making board, both light and strong. I can send you our starter pack of modelling tools which will be quite enough for you to recreate the Relief Plate," said Beth, "and if things go well, I can then suggest how you can transfer your finished wax replica plate into a more permanent sculpture."

A few evenings later after supper and sitting in his favourite chair with the large cake board on his lap, he worked the block of wax in his hands until the warmth made it malleable and as per the Tiranti instructions leaflet, began to spread the wax evenly across the board.

Ann, somewhat apprehensively, had inspected the wax and had decided its nature would not leave bits and pieces on the seat, if he was careful, nor was there any smell from the wax and so as she said, "You will not have to go in to the shed to work on the exercise."

Using the photo of his grandfather holding his trophy that Joseph had been able to get enlarged without leaving out too much of the detail of the animals all around the plaque, over the next three weeks working with enthusiasm most evenings, Joseph felt he had made a fair facsimile of the Award trophy and with support from Ann and his daughters, felt it was time to call Beth to see how he could turn the relief into something more permanent he could keep in his grandfather's name.

Joseph also found that the stimulating sculpturing activity was something he looked forward to in the day and to his surprise he realised that he found the task of replicating the plaque easy and came naturally to him, so he decided he must indeed have some artistic ability.

Joseph became so interested in pursuing his grandfather's project that ten days later he made an arranged visit to Tiranti in London to meet Beth and discuss the options for using hot wax relief as a model for a more permanent sculpture.

Beth seemed rather proud of her new customer and took Joseph to the Cold Casting Department where he was shown how to take a silicone rubber mould from the wax sculpture without damaging the wax and when the two part silicone had hardened remove it, which now left an exact cavity mould precise in every detail to his modelling, down to stray hairs, should he inadvertently leave any on his wax.

Joseph was then fascinated to be shown a bronze cold cast process using the mould where Polyester Resin was mixed with a catalyst and bronze metal powder added. As the operator explained, the metal powder particles are heavier than the polyester resin and drop to the bottom of the mould so that when the resin has hardened the complete sculpture can be removed from the mould and metal wool scrubbing on the finished surface leaves a bronze finish on the finished sculpture.

Joseph's mind was filled with the process he was learning about and he acquired the silicone wax kits to make his own mould for his grandfather's plaque.

Joseph now found tea and lunch breaks were opportunities for like-minded members of the distribution company to discuss their artistic projects and there were several occupying their free time and only too interested to share their experiences and listen to others with artistic projects of their own, all helping to lighten their working day.

It was in this way that Joseph was asked by Fred why he hadn't considered making a metal replica of his wax plaque now that he had a mould.

Fred, the company's electrical and mechanical site manager, explained it should be possible to cast the plaque in copper as a permanent memorial to Joseph's grandfather without too much trouble and a bit of background knowledge on how the process worked. Fred enthusiastically volunteered his time and knowledge to see if they could get a result.

The next few weeks during evenings and time at the weekend became a whole new experience for Joseph as Fred helped him put a small tank in his garden shed, a converted fish tank, and purchase a second hand Rectifier to convert AC current to DC, which Fred explained was necessary to get the copper particles to leave the copper bar in the cyanide solution in the tank and travel to the cavity mould, suspended the other end of the tank. All managed by the negative to positive attractions in the electrical world in which Joseph found himself immersed.

Somehow the daily work activity despite its rather soulless screen domination, no longer pressed down on Joseph's thoughts.

Mr Simons said to him several months into the new job.

"Splendid you really have settled into the new job and have improved our supply situation into the warehouse no end, well done."

The only 'fly in the ointment' artistically was that short of making a new mould from the wax relief out of a different material, other than silicone rubber, that Joseph found was inert and was not itself conductive and so even with a carefully made wire conductor all abound and over the mould in the plating bath, no copper would attach itself to the cavity mould, try as Joseph certainly did.

It was early one Saturday morning when he was polishing his black office shoes, it occurred to Joseph to wonder if there was any carbon in the wax which Joseph had learned was electrically conductive.

One thing led to another and a few evenings later, Joseph found himself with a tin of carbon powder brushing it into his grandfather's plaque activity mould and was delighted to find it stuck beautifully to his silicone rubber, leaving a conductive black coating all over and up to the copper wire surround.

Into the tank and a few hours later Joseph had a fine copper lining that he was able to strengthen with polyester resin, creating a permanent copper replica of his Grandfather's award.

The replica plaque in polished copper was much admired and Ann suggested he send a photograph of the piece of art history to the award promoters for their interest.

So Joseph sent a photograph and was excited to receive a letter from the Chairman asking if there was any chance of having a copper casting as given to his grandfather for their historic records to be put on permanent display.

Handing over the plaque with Ann at the Art Award sponsors offices, Joseph was thrilled to be asked by the Chairman if he could possibly design and cast the award for that year's Successful Sculpture exhibition.

Looking at his grandfather's copper replica on the wall at home that evening, Joseph somehow knew his wise grandfather was patting him on the back.

Finding His Sea Legs

Tommy pushed his face further into the pillow as his father pulled open his bedroom blinds.

"Come on, it's time to move, it's nearly ten and we have a date in Portsmouth Harbour."

"Oh, aw… do I have to, Dad. I have a terrible head," groaned Tommy.

"Yes we do. I have left the Alka-Seltzer there on the side and you will be fine when you have showered. I assume you had a good time. Your mother said you were singing loudly when Frank dropped you at the front door at two-thirty, so she is still in bed and I suggest for your sake we leave before she gets up!"

The drive down to the Marina in Portsmouth Harbour was undertaken, largely in silence, as Tommy gradually cleared his foggy head and tried to convince himself it had been a good idea to promise to support his dad on the trip when he'd received the invitation to look over the British America's Cup yacht entry which was undertaking its final fit-out and trials in the Marina at Portsmouth. It was an invitation from one of his dad's old sailing friends who Tommy remembered his dad saying was one of the design team for the British entry for the famous yacht race.

Tommy enjoyed his times with his dad. It was just that on this occasion his head wasn't travelling with him this morning and his own passionate interest in Formula 1 racing and rally cars was not going to be connected much today walking around a sailing boat.

Recovering steadily as the miles went by his mood improved and Tommy thought, '*Dad will love poking around the yacht and I can't count the number of times he has ferried me to motor things.*'

Having convinced himself this was his dad's day, Tommy began to think that when he went off to Bath University Engineering Department these trips were bound to become less frequent, and with his plans for his life working in engineering, perhaps even having his own creative engineering company, he really must enjoy his time with his dad while he still lived at home.

Thinking ahead helped Tommy to clear his head and so by the time the car drew up at the security gate at the entrance to Portsmouth Marina, Tommy felt ready to face the day.

His father showed the policeman the letter of invitation, who then directed them to a fenced off area with a gate leading to a row of large yachts moored to a quay.

Tommy and his dad were courteously asked to park the car and walk through the protected gatehouse where they both signed in under the careful scrutiny of yet another guard until they could finally walk down to where a huge yacht with its towering mast, was moored.

Tommy's dad hurried ahead and shook hands warmly with a grey haired, sunburned, man in a blue jersey with America's Cup logo proudly emblazoned across his chest.

"Hi Tommy, don't suppose you remember me. I'm George. I remember you when you had your first tricycle. Now here you are soon off to an Engineering University and your dad says your ambition is to go engineering and motor rallying. Good for you, you don't want to follow your dad and spend time on a racing yacht, being sick over the side."

Both men laughed. "That only happened once," said Tommy's dad, "and George only just survived that cross channel race as I recall."

"Come aboard," said George. "Now I'm afraid you will have put those shoe overrides on. Mr Langdale, our sponsor, is most particular about the decking, and as a matter of fact, Tommy, the polished condition of the deck can materially affect the speed of the yacht through the water."

George continued, "As your interest is Formula 1 race cars, I am sure you already know a good deal about the aerodynamic values of design on those cars. It's just the same on a racing yacht like this."

"Now mind where you go; this trimaran is built as slim as the design will allow in order to give the yacht the strength necessary to get her through the water, pretty rough water at times when we are making real speed, in your language Tommy as much as fifty miles per hour."

"Crickey," said Tommy, "that is impressive."

"Well take a look up at the mast, Tommy," George said pointing upwards.

Tommy stretched his neck backwards, peering upwards along the polished black mast towering above him to the stays and supporting geometry of the frame necessary to manage the huge sail.

George read Tommy's question before he had a chance to ask it.

"The mast has to support a sixty-two foot virtually rigid sail. That, Tommy, is an area as big as the wing of a Boeing 777 airliner. Just imagine the stresses on the boat with the sea holding us back while the huge sail is pushing the yacht through the water race lines when the yacht is swinging through angles of twenty five degrees or more."

Tommy was fascinated. "Will the yacht tip over in difficult conditions?

"Well, this is why we have a trimaran design, a central section with the two big float expansions. Look there Tommy, you can see the support structure either side, even though the floats are underwater. When she gets going and lifts up two or three metres then the buoyancy is balanced, although I suspect personally that at top speed and executing a sharp turn she could be vulnerable to turn over leaving us all dangling on our straps!" He and Tommy's dad laughed.

Continuing his explanation George said, "We will only find out in the trials off the Isle of Wight when the sponsors will be watching us next month. So let's hope it doesn't happen or they might think their millions of pounds sponsorship had been wasted.

Of course Tommy they know, like every America's Cup yacht sponsor, there are lots of PR advantages and in our case new equipment testing which can be invaluable for worldwide yacht design. Then of course there is the prestige of being the owner of a winning America's Cup yacht. Lots of TV interviews, meeting the President and Prime Minister, the sponsors like that."

George led Tommy and his dad towards the centre of the yacht where the entry below deck was situated.

"This will interest the engineer in you, Tommy. This yacht is a sloop rigged boat and is virtually all built out of carbon fibre and epoxy resin, which makes her so light and gives her the strength she needs in all weathers and the ability to get to speeds as much as twice the speed of the wind that drives her, bearing in mind she is ninety feet long and each of her two booms are a third as long as she is… quite a lady," George said proudly.

Tommy was more and more fascinated by the yacht as they returned from crawling between the interior of the bulkhead below deck and as his interest was caught by a technician fitting a piece of electronic equipment on the aft of the yacht close to the rudder mechanism, he turned to George and enquired.

"What is that technician fitting to that piece of gear?"

"You may well ask," said George. "That electronic box films all the race activities, timing everything and ensuring that we do not cut corners or miss any of the positioning buoys which we have to navigate.

That 'bloody spy', as we call it, has to come off and a replacement installed after each leg, and as everyone is as busy as hell it's a difficult job. You can see it has to be bolted on to the stainless steel bracket to ensure it is not shot overboard in heavy seas or swept off when we get a big wave hit."

Tommy went over and talked to the operator fitting the box while his dad and George reminisced about old sailing adventures.

As Tommy watched the technician fitting the stainless steel pins, an idea occurred to him and fishing out the pad he always carried in his back pocket for engineering ideas, he sketched out the box, and with the help of the friendly technician noted the dimensions of the electronic box and the bracket.

All the way home and over the next two days Tommy was completely absorbed by the 'spy' electronic box fitting, his engineering instincts knowing that there had to be a simpler method of retaining and changing the unit.

Sitting in his bedroom with the floor covered in papers with half ideas and calculations, he finally decided on a two part snap-locking hinge which could use the electronic box flanges and hook firmly on to the stainless steel retaining bracket, no matter what the shock and vibration the yacht might experience during the race.

Tommy's dad went off on a business trip for a few days and so Tommy, full of inventor excitement, decided that rather than wait to share his idea with his father, he would send his design off to George, using the address on the invitation they had received to visit the racing yacht.

A few days later Tommy received a long letter from George which he did show to his dad.

The letter opened with enthusiastic congratulations for Tommy's snap-lock hinge, letting him know his engineers had built a model to the drawings and it had worked perfectly, reducing the change over time for the electronic monitoring unit to a matter of seconds rather than minutes, and letting Tommy know that the America's Cup component supply company had immediately taken up the design and were producing the component for the whole fleet of yachts.

Tommy and his dad sat together with the letter as it dawned on Tommy in his haste to show his invention, he had missed a real commercial opportunity.

Tommy's dad said, "Look, son, this is a great lesson learned. What this proves is you have a really creative engineering brain and the experience will be invaluable as you develop your career, so that when your next creative idea is formulated you will give all the commercial possibilities proper consideration before you launch forth."

"Now let's put a letter together to George, getting him to get the component manufacturer to acknowledge your engineering creativity in designing for what is now their snap-lock device. That will look well on your CV when you go looking for your first engineering job and who knows perhaps they will be honourable and send you a bob or two for your invention?"

The Partnership Budget

Jonathan unlocked the tin box and lifted the battered lid, looking down at the pile of tissue paper covered prints inside. Carefully he wrote on the sheet pasted inside the lid against the blank entry numbered sixteen, Fatteri copy of the work in the Modern Art Gallery Florence.

Jonathan slid the 30x24cm lithograph out of its protective envelope and enjoyed several minutes looking again at the lithograph copy of the painting before wrapping it in tissue paper and placing it on top of the other fifteen lithographs lying in the tin trunk.

Jonathan carefully wrote against the detail on entry sixteen, 'Purchased December 2015 £250' and looked once again at the list of Italian artists, Den Chirico, and others all with their lithographed paintings. He mentally calculated the purchase value now at more than Five thousand pounds, thinking as he did so 'just as well Cyril had no idea how much I have invested in my little collection over the three years of their relationship'.

Jonathan locked the battered tin trunk and pocketed the key, smiling as he caught sight of the key label 'Gym Locker', another small subterfuge to make sure Cyril never got wind of the investments he made in his collection.

Jonathan walked out of their cluttered garage, stacked with boxes and unwanted furniture to such an extent that their two cars had to sit on the drive way of the small cottage they shared, consoling himself he could at least enjoy the collection when Cyril is on his 'learn how to paint' away days.

'After all', thought Jonathan, 'it's thanks to my job at the bank our savings account is growing towards the day when we can afford to invest in a larger property, with proper garaging for the cars, and having the money to move and set up home in the style in which our relationship could now feel comfortable'.

Cyril was positively bouncing with excitement in the kitchen as Jonathan came through the back door.

"Look at this house here," he said, stabbing at the property section of the local rag.

"That's the very bungalow I was telling you about. The one I visited a while ago when the owner had been in the shop to ask about new curtains. Well they must have decided to move on and the place is up for rent again. We have to go and look at it. You will love the space and we would have a garden."

"OK, OK, course we will visit, you fix it up but please remember this is my busy time with everyone wanting their year-end accounts so check with me when the agents offer a time for us to visit." Jonathan was studying the picture of a neat bungalow with an integral two car garage. "But look, Cyril, we are going to use the garage for our cars so you are going to have to grit your teeth and get rid of some of the collection of stuff you have piled up in our garage here."

The visit to the rental bungalow went smoothly despite Cyril's long list of decorative changes he felt essential to make the place 'liveable', whilst Jonathan's concern on the central heating efficiency, the insulation, window fittings and general services were mostly put aside after his checks on their condition.

The agent was insistent that there was a queue of potential leasers wanting to take on the property and he claimed the owners were extremely interested in any tenant who could take on the lease as quickly as possible as they did not want to leave the property vacant.

The arrangements suited Jonathan and Cyril, who had a month's notice arrangement with their present home and both felt this was the right time for them to take on the challenge of moving. Cyril somewhat anxious, if excited, by the need he felt to make changes to the décor and drapes made his list without according to Jonathan any concern over the costs, while Jonathan was confident that with proper pre-planning in the month they could move and fit in all their existing furniture into the bungalow without breaking the budget.

When Jonathan gave Cyril his list of tasks and timescales, it caused Cyril to put on one of his 'fit of the vapours' performances, but over a hug and a bottle of excellent Merlot, "Which," as Jonathan said, "they would not at least now have to move," the couple agreed their individual plans for the coming month.

Jonathan's long working and travel day in the bank inevitably left tasks to Cyril, despite Jonathan's misgivings. One of these was clearing and disposing of unwanted items stored in their garage.

Cyril's contacts in the furnishing trade were useful over this matter and with the emphasis from Jonathan, "get the best prices possible but shift all the items we have agreed should go and make sure you get someone who understands the value of the Victorian table and chairs and that old chest on chest with the brass handles. That must have some antique value."

A short time later Cyril was in a high state of excitement when Jonathan returned from the office.

"Look at the cheque I received from the antique and collectable specialist who took everything away today. You were right the chest on chest was quite valuable."

Jonathan looked at the cheque and said, "Well done, Cyril, that's much more than I had thought the things were worth. Let me see the list." He then studied the lengthy list of details until his eye caught 'Ex-Military Gurkha Officer's Travel Black Tin Box'.

Appalled Jonathan gasped in horrified tones. "The black tin was one of the things I specifically said we should keep. What… why on earth would you have let it go?" Conscious as he said it, he could not bring himself to admit to Cyril his secret collection of the lithographs, let alone admit to the amount of their joint income he had been channelling into the collection, horrified that the antique specialist had walked away with a significant bonus hidden in the battered box.

Jonathan then said, scarcely able to breathe, "How much did he give you for the tin box?"

Cyril checked his notes. "Oh only twenty pounds, the dealer thought when he had cleaned the box up a bit and identified the military history from the label inside, it would make fifty pounds in the right sale."

Jonathan groaned and tried to work out, with his head swimming, how he was going to work out a way of explaining the reality of the now lost hidden collection to Cyril.

Beaming Cyril then said, "Well, Jonathan, I have been saving this surprise up for you. When the antique specialist was looking all the things over he asked about the old tin box and I said I thought you wanted to keep it because it belonged to your Uncle. He said, 'Fine, out of interest let me see if it is what I think a military officer's box should be.' He had a key collection for all sorts of cabinets and guess what, he opened the box up."

With Jonathan stunned by the loss of his collection, quite unable to speak, Cyril left the room to return carrying a beautiful polished oak box and opening it he said.

"Jonathan your Uncle must have been collecting these prints for years and the antique guy said they are very valuable and he let me have this lovely box for you to keep so

I thought you might like to continue to add to your uncle's collection when we get settled into our new place… a new hobby."

Jonathan was far too overcome with emotion to say anything as he hugged Cyril in thanks and relief.

Cyril looked over Jonathan's shoulder and smiled, in a knowing sort of way!

A Family Business

Jeremy (known usually as 'Jerry') reviewed his eighteenth birthday with his friend Vince in the Costa coffee house, over a latte coffee which Jeremy stated had a fourteen percent cost of the selling price, a worthwhile profit to the coffee house, he observed. A constant moan of his when he used his considerable calculating skills and statistic interests to show off his not inconsiderable irritation with the world in which he lived, a negative world that according to him was unfair as he listed the burdens he saw himself saddled with in this the first day of his nineteenth year.

All matters which Vince, sitting opposite him, took with a pinch of salt, having heard the growing list in varying degrees of 'unfairness' after each birthday over the previous five years, virtually the whole time they had been close friends.

At the beginning of their friendship soon after he was fifteen Vince, who admired Jerry's frequently made observations on the fairness, or unfairness, of events that touched them both as they battled families and the school system with their mutually disliked year teacher and their mutual lack of sporting skills, it became clear to him as he got to know Jerry's family that most of Jerry's perverse views of life and independence stemmed from the fact that Jerry's sisters disliked him. They saw him as an unwanted addition to the family having arrived unexpectedly some years after the arrival of the two talented sisters, who were the cherished stars in his parents' eyes. Who had to be indulged in every way to encourage them to achieve the high academic standard that would inevitably lead to significant professional success in their chosen future careers?

An expectation that Vince saw was being realised as both girls had left school, one into hairdressing and the other into the local veterinary service, and despite some hope from his father and mother for their son to enter a profession, perhaps as an Accountant, Jerry floated disconsolately through his schooling failing to achieve the entry standard for university, even in maths where his numeracy had been expected at least by his maths master to give him a shot at entry.

Jerry's failures although commented on regularly by the family, did not bother him greatly as he had no wish to spend four years at any university and the scholastic performance had in the end not surprised his parents who had given up anticipating a career for him based upon any academic achievements. Indeed as his rather negative and difficult teenage attitudes had developed, his parents had even given up the thought that Jerry might make a contribution to the family bicycle repair and sales business in the town.

As Jerry went on to explain to Vince over the birthday coffee review.

"I have realised my two 'witch' like sisters have been putting me down for years with my parents just to make sure they get all the perks and attention as they manipulate their way through life. I only found out quite by chance when I visited the shop and saw a letter from the family lawyer in my dad's office, the family had raised the thought that the high street shop site freehold could be converted into a house and would go equally to my two miserable sisters and I when my parents have passed on. Well, you know what that means?"

"No, not really," said Vince, thinking rather more if he could afford another coffee.

"Well obviously, the 'witches' are planning to sell the site as a building development without having to take my views into account once the parents are gone. You can bet the shop value will be peanuts compared to the value of the house or office development right in the centre of the town."

Taking a gulp of his coffee Jerry continued. "And another thing to annoy me about those two conniving women, do you know I found the two of them had complained to my dad about the money I have been wasting on my coin collection! 'Wasting on buying more old coins' I heard one of them grumbling to dad. What has it got to do with them? If I was spending my allowance or birthday money on drugs or booze they might have a case but my coin collection! They will go to any length to keep me in a bad light with my parents."

"I think they are manipulating to get me out of the house now I'm nineteen. I think my mum is unhappy about the way things are going but she won't say anything that might upset her 'two amazing daughters' who are going to have the careers she can brag about in her ladies' circle."

Jerry looked at Vince and said, "It's alright for you being the 'one and only' in your family."

"Ugh, forget it," said Vince, "it's not all milk and honey when you are the only one for your parents to plant all their ambitions on, particularly with my crap school record and disappointing my dad that I never made any of the school soccer teams."

"OK, come on," said a now clearly discouraged Vince. "Let's go. We're going to miss any good stuff in the car boot sale if we don't get a move on and," he added slapping his pocket, "I have that seven quid just in case I can find another classic management book to add to my collection, which by the way by my last reckoning, is now worth six hundred quid in the right sale. Beside which," he continued, "I enjoy getting the ideas from how management developed in the fifties and sixties, a real boom time in the UK, so that when I get going I will have a plan to build up my business."

Pushing through the coffee door, Jerry said, "You're more likely to be running a stall in the market than being the next Richard Branson, but you're right, let's go

We might get lucky today. What's this the fifth car boot sale and all we have found or could afford was that book you picked up on 'Marketing Strategies' for entry into the British Empire. Not much use in today's world, I should have thought."

And with this said they left the coffee shop to cycle to the field some two miles out of the town.

The field was already filled with cars and vans cluttered with the unwanted residue of families domestic items of every style and material creation, with the scars and scuffs on everything from the previous Christmas unwanted gifts to items lying for many years in the back of the garage.

As experienced visitors to car boot sales Jerry and Vince padlocked their bicycles together around a convenient fence post before undertaking a preliminary tour of the open backed vans and car boots, marking the regular traders who knew what they were doing in order to make a living, from the amateur punters who Jerry liked to spot, who might have a few coins he could pick up well below their market value.

Jerry's coin collecting interest was tailed to his lack of funds and despite occasionally pushing the 'boat out' for an English coin earlier than the George VI period, his growing collection fell mainly into this milled coin era, although not infrequently he found a George VI penny worth having amongst a collection of low, or no value, coins from many countries and he had been quite successful putting together small collections of coins from their respected centres and getting the local dealer in the town, who liked Jerry and also liked to support a budding coin enthusiast, to take them into his shop with a small margin of profit for Jerry's hours touring car boot sites.

The boot sale was disappointing for the two with nothing much to show for an hour of crisscrossing the site, other than a growing feeling of dampness and dishevelment from the persistent driving rain which had arrived as they chained their bicycles to the post.

Stopping to consider if this was the moment to cycle home, the boys were standing under the raised awning over the rear doors of a small van. The owner came up to enquire if there was anything in his range of boxes, wooden, plastic and cardboard filling the van and on the grass under the awning that interested them.

Jerry explained their separate interests adding politely that they had taken a close look when they started the tour without seeing anything of interest.

The van owner recognised a couple of young boot sale enthusiasts when he saw them and chatted friendly to them rather proudly explaining he had just done a nice trade on a large silver salver, taking in a bag of English coins as well as cash for the transaction from a, "Gentleman who had no interest in the coins but wanted the silver salver to present 'as Captain' he said to his Golf Club."

The dealer spread out the assorted fifty or so copper coins which they both looked over briefly, the one or two ten pence and other coins that Jerry knew would not fetch much more than their face value with his friendly coin dealer but when the trader said, "Look, I have had a good day, do you want to take the lot off my hands for twenty pounds," he agreed, and the two cycled home damp but Jerry at least weighed down slightly on one side with his bag of coins.

Back at home Jerry found his mother and sisters gathered around the kitchen with his father, looking grey and anxious and he repeated what he had just told the rest of the family.

"Jerry, I have just returned from the bank with my accountant. It looks as if the family cycle business is going to have to close. Goodness knows what my dad would be saying if he was here now." He shook his head sadly.

"I am sorry I have not been talking about the problems over the last couple of years but I had hoped to see an upturn in sales and the maintenance work recover but times are difficult and I'm sorry to say I haven't adjusted very well with the changes and the bank are about to pull the plug on our overdraft now it's up to ten thousand pounds."

Mr Fothergill, the accountant, says there is not a lot I can do as we have at least five more years before we have paid off the mortgage on this house. I know the girls had thoughts about the shop as a unit that could be developed as a home or office but I have looked into this and getting a change of use planning consent would take several years, and you all know there are plenty of empty shops in the high street right now. I honestly don't know what to do."

With this Jerry's dad put his head in his hands.

"Come on, dear, we are all in this together. Now I'm going to make us all a nice up of tea," said Jerry's mum.

Later Jerry walked round to Vince's house and sitting in his bedroom, ran through the disturbing news he had been given in his parents' kitchen.

To his surprise Vince took a line he had not expected.

"I am not surprised," he said. "I have been thinking for ages your dad wasn't following the cycle trends. Let me show what I have been practicing my marketing programmes on, with your dad's shop in mind."

This said Vince opened up his iPad and having located the site, showed Jerry a series of cycles the design of which Jerry had not seen around the town.

"See the shape of this bike," said Vince. "Streamlined, look at the tyres, see how slim the saddle support is and look at the shape of the saddle. See that unit on the primary support. You know why all this is possible? Carbon fibre, super strong and light. See this cycle in this shot, I guarantee you could hook your finger on the cross bar here and pick that bicycle up, even in your dodgy condition."

Vince enthusiastically continued. "Another line is the new electric powered bike, super for the hilly roads around here. They would be a real attraction for the older cyclist."

"Yes that's all very well," said jerry, "but these machines have to be horrendously expensive."

"No, not really," said Vince. "Coming down all the time. Your dad could fix up an agency to bring them in from China and get promoting them to the cycle groups in this country. A bit of advertising, newspaper items, etc."

"Marketing," said Vince, getting on to his favourite subject. "I have roughed out a programme for your dad to circulate all the cycle clubs and if he gets the sort of response to these new cycles I would expect, he could place a significant order and move on from the sit-up-and-beg cycles that you and I and most everyone are currently struggling with."

"Yes but," said Jerry before Vince continued.

"No 'buts'. Let me finish, cos this could be my start in business too. You see if your dad could get the new marketing picture then he could bring in light weight helmets, and lycra cycle clothes that are being produced in France and all sorts of cycle accessories."

"Well, honestly Vince you really have a hell of an argument here. Well, OK, OK, I meant a marketing concept – sorry, but look dad says his company is in immediate big, big, financial trouble. I mean, right now, so all this marketing stuff is just never going to be brought in."

Later that evening Jerry was sitting in his bedroom sorting through his new bag of copper coins and putting aside any he thought might interest his friendly coin dealer. He found a sequence of nineteen-thirty pieces, so glad to be away from the rest of the family in the kitchen, sunk in depressed discussions about their future.

Even his sisters were being nice to him as everyone gave their support to their very worried dad.

Jerry took his new packet of old English coins into the coin dealer and spent a bit of time over a mug of tea sharing some of the family worries and suggesting he might need to bring in the whole of his collection and get what he could as the family were going to need all the money they could get their hands on.

The dealer was looking through the coins on his green blaze inspection tray and suddenly stopped listening to Jerry and went over to his row of reference books before carefully inspecting a penny with the eyeglass magnifier.

Jerry's tale of woe had dried up and the agent said, "Just sit there for a minute Jerry. I want to talk to a friend of mine about this penny."

He disappeared into his back office while Jerry wondered what it was all about.

The dealer bustled back into the shop.

"Jerry, I have a surprise for you. This 1933 penny is extremely rare as none were circulated that year and very, very few were coined. You own one. I have just talked to my good friend at Sprinks, he says at auction this coin will make at least fifty thousand pounds."

Jerry sat there with his mouth open.

"Now if you are in agreement, I will act as your agent. I would normally handle a sale of 10 per cent of the value but for you let's say 5 per cent. If you're in agreement I will put in place the arrangements for the sale at SPINKS or next month to give them time to arrange to promote this very rare coin."

The dealer continued in an excited but measured tone.

"If you agree I will have the legal papers for you this afternoon and I suggest they will cause the bank to hold off until the money is to hand, normally that would be seven days."

Back at home having collected Vince and recovered from the shock of events, Jerry outlined the drama to his stunned family, finishing with, "If you agree dad I will pass over the funds to settle the overdraft. Then if you also agree, Vince can help you with the marketing of carbon fibre and electric powered bikes and you girls can help dad with a range of cycle clothing. I'm sure between us all we will make Grandpa proud of our family business."

The Inventor

Luke slammed his briefcase down on the kitchen table and switched on the electric kettle before he dumped himself down on the stool.

"Hard day, dear?" enquired his grandmother, Joan, peeling potatoes in the sink for supper.

"Honestly, Gran, I don't know why I bother. They give you a 'concept' that needs an engineering solution, and you know how many evenings I have been working on the idea," said Luke as he pulled a wooden and tin foil frame model from his bag and put it on the table.

"There, that is a working field water pump which would definitely work in those flooded African fields after heavy rain. What that …!" He held himself back from illustrating his engineering tutor, Henry Biggins, name with an expletive, knowing perfectly well his grandmother strongly disapproved of his lapses.

"*That might be all very well in the pub Luke but not in the house please,*" she frequently said, frowning at him.

Joan inspected the awkward looking assembly of leavers and wheels as Luke once again explained how the force of the flood water passing by would cause the water scoops to lift up water and deposit it into bamboo pipes to be evacuated from the site of the flood.

"And, Gran, I am sure hundreds of these cheap to produce 'lift pumps' could be moved easily to the flooded growing fields and then moved on to the next flood area but not according to that blithering idiot Biggins. He would just say."

'Nice idea Luke but impractical for the native community to put together and build, just a little too complicated.'

Luke gritted his teeth as he continued to report what his tutor had said.

'The concept Joe and Ben have come up with is I believe the best idea we have giving us a solution to the project I set you.'

"Never mind, dear, you did your best and I am sure you are right." Luke's grandmother said as she turned from the sink to giving him a supportive smile.

"You know it's often a matter of persisting with an idea when you believe in it, never mind what the critics say. Now could you move your model off the table so I can set the table for supper please? By the way have you written that letter to your mother? It's no good you making that face and I know she has disappointed you in lots of ways, but she is your mother and her new partner does not make it easy for her to come down to see you. Now you are eighteen and you will soon have your Engineering Degree, then a real job and goodness knows what else, you know we have always agreed this will be your real home, haven't we?"

Luke got up and went over and hugged his grandmother.

"Of course you're right and I will always live with you, you know that and I will drop my mother a line, tonight."

Good to his word Luke wrote his letter and with a stamp from his grandmother, posted it on the way down to the pub that evening.

Settled into his favourite corner of the bar with his mate, Jerry, who shared many of his interests including motors and girls, neither of which they could afford or were fortunate enough to have more than a distant interest in!

During their usual discussion on various matters over a pint, the bar chat was suspended, as it was routinely, by the incoming arrival of a 747 just over the chimney pots on its way into Heathrow from Bangalore or Budapest!

Once the racket and the rattle of the bar glasses had subsided, Jerry observed.

"It's bloody amazing someone hasn't found a way of cutting out some of the engine noise, since they are never going to move the airport."

Later that night Luke, watching a late night movie without interest, found himself reflecting upon Jerry's words in an absent minded way whilst spinning his locker key ring around his finger, the keys spinning out around his finger as he did so, when he found himself concentrating on what he was doing and as he did so a thought struck him.

No sooner had the idea come to him than he swung around to his desk and sliding a pad of paper in front of him, he started to translate ideas to paper.

In no time at all he had a circular structure drawn with a series of protruding vanes extending around the edge. Then with a red pen he illustrated a jet of flame through the circular ring, most of the lines he drew passing straight through the ring but a percentage of his red gas lines on the cdge being deflected outwards at a right angle from the main jet.

By midnight, Luke had checked enough expanded gas details on his laptop to be sure that the environmental air influenced by the burned fuel evacuated from the exhaust orifice of a jet aircraft engine, not only provided the forward energy for the plane, but also created the sound waves which when they reached the ground caused the sound that those under the flight path had to live with.

By one o'clock, Luke had convinced himself that if he could deflect a percentage of the heat gas away from the main thrust of the jet engine, there would be a reduction in the sound footprints passing over the ground.

Luke became both excited and determined to present and prove his idea as his end of course 'Creative Concept' paper required for every student by the formidable Mr Biggins as the end of year exercise.

The following morning at breakfast Luke explained his idea to his grandmother which helped him focus upon some of the things he needed to do to prove out his idea. Joan delayed him going out to the garden shed workshop with the promise she would come up with the money for him to buy a blow lamp and some sort of sound detecting unit from the list he had prepared.

"You can go out and find the items today, then you should take this idea to bed and sleep on it to make sure it sounds as good to you tomorrow morning because you look like the wreck of the Hesperus right now!"

Sure enough well before breakfast the next morning Luke felt just as positive about his idea and in his workshop he gathered the items on his bench to help him prove out his theory.

His grandmother, as always, insisted on breakfast and in this he was joined by Jerry who had been summoned by mobile to join them at breakfast and offer assistance with the project

Jerry arrived with a limited enthusiasm for being Luke's assistant but he knew how good the breakfasts were!

Luke had been able to buy for ten pounds a hand held sound level meter which had been used for a demonstration. The music centre manager confidently

confirming he would be able to monitor sound up to 120 decibels as close as he liked to stand to the band.

Luke made no attempt to explain the real purpose of his purchase.

In the workshop the two boys began to build the model airplane jet engine flame evacuation unit with a stainless steel ring, hacksawed out after they had carefully measured, at a careful distance, the width of the blowlamp flame.

By lunchtime despite all the bracket and hinges in Luke's large collection of bits and pieces, they were still some way from a full trial and had not even started to make the twenty or so tear drop shaped fan blades that Luke hoped when assembled on to the inside of the ring would spin off a percentage of the expended exhaust gas and flame.

Lunch gave the boys a chance to review matters and Jerry, who Mr Biggins had declared to his embarrassment to the whole class '*had a tidy mind*', insinuating thereby the majority were without this advantage, started that afternoon to draft out an assembly schedule and concept overview. Essential ingredients as the project was to be Luke's end of syllabus submission.

With the end of his engineering course rapidly approaching, Luke worked early and late to complete his tests and with Jerry's help carefully recorded each step in a way which he hoped would be marked sufficiently highly to give him his diploma.

The tests did prove that the sound wave effect was dissipated by his spinning disk, although many of his sound readings were somewhat subjective.

A month later at the diploma award ceremony with his grandmother and mother in the audience, Luke's name was called after the high achievers with distinctions as one of the students who had achieved a pass.

As was his wont Mr Biggins commented on each student, '*just to embarrass the parents*' was Jerry's view and therefore commented on Luke's project in a most conciliatory tone.

"Whilst Luke has shown a considerable aptitude for creativity, it is hoped he will concentrate upon more practical matters in his engineering course."

"Never mind, dear," said Joan later to a rather subdued Luke. "Now we really do have to concentrate on getting a job and although you have that interview at the garden tractor repairers, I have another idea."

And this said she produced the name and address of the Development Director for Rolls Royce Engines in Derby.

"I think you should send your project papers to him, you really have nothing to lose."

A couple of weeks later an official embossed letter from the Rolls Royce Company arrived for Luke and to his surprise and excitement the letter was from the Personnel Manager and it read.

'Dear Luke,

The Development Director has asked me to write to you having seen your engineering idea and since your letter we have been able to check with your training college on your other creative programmes whilst you were completing your diploma and we are pleased to offer you a role in our Engineering Development team here at Derby as soon as it might be convenient for you to join us.'

'Providing you are interested in the opportunity, could you complete the enclosed forms and you will be sent the full details, salary, etc.'

When both Luke and Joan had dried their eyes and stopped hugging each other, Luke said.

"I wonder what Mr Biggins is going to say when I tell him at the leaving party, I have a job at Rolls Royce!

Seeing the Reality of the Situation

The shop doorbell rang and Francis Wells threw down his gilding brush in irritation as he took his spectacles off and undid his blue striped 'butcher's apron', planted it on a stool before he took the steep staircase down to the shop below.

"Good afternoon, can I be of assistance?" he addressed the lady and gentleman standing in front of a large mirror, resplendent with its heavy figured relief, the gilding catching the afternoon sun pouring through the shop front windows.

The lady surveyed Frank as in much the same way she would a door-to-door cleaning product salesman. His family insisted in calling him Frank despite his liking his mother's insistence that he was Francis back in Ireland.

"We are interested in a large mirror for our front hall," the lady said, in a false cultured voice.

At this point her rather overweight and florid husband chimed in.

"Of course depending on the price of these gold versions." And with this he motioned with his arm to the twenty or so framed mirrors hanging on the walls of the shop.

"Well," said Frank, well used to the husband versus wife approach.

"It rather depends upon which of the gilded frames." He dwelt on the word 'gilded' giving it a quality connotation that a normal mirror frame could never have.

"The one you are looking at has a frame moulded from patterns we hold here made a hundred years ago. Oh, and incidentally, madam, since you clearly have a good eye, we recently framed an oil painting using the moulds for the Royal Academy in London.

'The Royal Academy'. The wife could clearly see ahead showing her new house visitors the mirror with a casual comment along the lines of, "Oh, we decided to get the mirror framed to match the Swiss Alps in winter hanging in the Royal Academy."

Her husband saw the mood change, spelling an above budget expense for their new place and struggling to exhibit some control he asked Frank.

"Well, yes, but how much is this particular mirror?"

Frank adopted his 'now to give comfort to the husband line'.

"Well, Mr...." He waited until he was told 'Carlisle'. "Well, Mr Carlisle, I can tell you in confidence that these bespoke gilded mirrors are currently appreciating at better than twenty percent a year. As I am sure you know with all this Brexit affecting the financial markets people of substance, such as yourselves, see investing in high value items so much more profitable than stocks and shares."

"Yes but," Mr Carlisle struggled on. "I'm sure it is a good investment but... how much is this gilded mirror?"

Frank adopted a slightly lower tone.

"Well, my people are out with customers this morning, which is why I have had the pleasure of meeting you both. Now where is your new home?"

Mrs Carlisle said rather proudly.

"We have just moved into Regent Crescent on the Cumberland Estate."

"Oh what a delightful area that is. One or two of my better clients have mirrors on the estate. Not as fine as this one I can assure you."

Frank moved next to the mirror.

"Now in the normal event this mirror would be placed at Five thousand pounds but in the circumstances with you living in such a prestigious location, I could agree a sale at Four thousand three hundred. Of course I would need to come over personally to size, place and install the mirror in your hall, and in view of your interest in cultural quality in the UK, I will waive my normal installation charge to have this fine example of our creative work placed in such a significant home."

Sometime later a slightly bemused Mr Carlisle led his delighted wife out of the shop, short of a cheque which would create a significant dent in his bank account, having spent at least three times what he had fondly thought was the agreed budget for the front hall mirror.

Frank walked back from his goodbyes at the shop door, stopping to regard himself in the gilded mirror now sporting a red sticker loudly pronouncing 'SOLD'.

"You're good, Francis, you're good," he muttered whilst preening himself and straightening his tie.

"Got that old touch and thank goodness I have got this over large mirror sold. The lads are going to bow down when I tell them how much I got for it. Just as well I shifted it with the move coming on."

He grimaced at himself in the mirror thinking, '*all these arrangements I have to complete to get into the new place. I really do not know how I'm going to find the time for the administration on top of all the new mirror work we are trying to deal with.*'

'*May be*' he mused '*I should not have let Clare go just for a few quid more. I could have done with her help now. Why is it these people want a pay rise as soon as they see the books?*

Oh well I suppose I can manage a bit of charm here and there, a couple of back-handers to the contractors to get things finished and we will be in the new place in no time.'

The meeting with the property agent's site manager, George Feather, was not one that played to Frank's confidence feeling that he could get events sorted in his favour.

George in his usual blunt Yorkshire way had a nasty habit of keeping notes of matters agreed and wheeling out his notebook and carefully slipping back the elasticated strap, he read out.

"On the seventeenth... that was June, Mr Wells," he continued. "Mr Wells informed me that he had a first class electrical contractor who would carry out the required electrical inside installation and link up to the Electricity Board's unit outside the site for one thousand five hundred pounds, and as the best quote I had obtained was three thousand six hundred pounds, it was agreed Mr Wells should proceed."

"Now, Mr Wells, you are telling me," George was carefully scribbling in his notebook, "that your contractor has found the work will cost considerably more."

He looked up at Frank expectantly.

"Well, yes, you see apparently he has a considerable workload and cannot do the job in the time that we had agreed," Frank finished lamely.

"Well I will talk to the contractors again, but even if they can adjust towards the original timescale, there is no way they will adjust the price for the job."

Only a matter of an hour later, Frank was in the new premises with the carpenter fitter trying to agree the assembly benches and the installation of a wall between the workshop and the showroom area.

"Yes I know I did not mention the stairs up to the first floor but honestly this is such a prestigious job for you, surely you can hold the price to include the little set of stairs. I can assure you all our clients will hear how excellent your firm has been in carrying out the work!"

As the day progressed issue followed issue. The gas piping had to enter the building at a different angle to accommodate Frank's layout for the equipment he needed for melting the casting material to go into any of the several hundred carved wooden moulds used to produce the bespoke mirror frames.

The estimate for the workshop light fittings arrived by mail and Frank thought they had added up the list to include the date, a figure well over his budget.

On top of the heavy blows to his confidence and the budget, Frank was called downstairs into the shop by Alice, his young workshop apprentice, to see a council planning officer.

Asking Alice to stay in the shop in case a customer turned up, Frank sat the council official down and asked him, rather anxiously, what his visit was all about.

"Well, Mr Wells, now that you are moving your assembly and shop to the other side of the road, my manager thought you ought to know we are planning to place a zebra crossing and lights across the road opposite your shop entrance."

Frank stared at him aghast.

"But why there? I mean I'm opening a prestigious showroom. I can't have a zebra crossing right in front. That would be awful."

"Sorry Mr Wells but this has been planned for some time. I am surprised the site owner's agent didn't mention it to you."

On his way back from seeing the council official out of the shop door, Frank stopped at the large gilded frame mirror, and looked at himself.

In a matter of two days he seemed to have aged twenty years. The sublime confidence of seeing himself as the successful salesman was now replaced by the image of someone he scarcely recognised, who was committed to a more than he could possibly afford new site which was going to look like somewhere down Balham Street Market which none of his clients from Tunbridge Wells would want to visit.

His despair was interrupted by Alice asking.

"Can I get you a mug of tea, Mr Wells? You are looking so pale?"

Frank accepted the mug of tea gratefully and sat down to try to recover his equilibrium. Alice sat opposite him and looked at him in a concerned way.

"The truth is Alice," said Frank. "This move over the road to the new site is proving to be much more expensive than I had planned or budgeted for and now the gentleman from the council has arrived to tell me they are going to put a zebra crossing right opposite our new shop door, can you just imagine all the people, children and dogs flowing past our shop front. It's going to put off our bespoke mirror customers and kill off any new customers."

Frank mopped his brow with his handkerchief.

"This whole move matter has got the better of me," he told Alice.

Alice regarded Frank carefully.

"May I speak freely, Mr Wells? She said.

"Of course Alice and please call me Frank, everyone else does."

"Well, Frank, I think you may be considering the situation the wrong way around. Like everyone in your team I have been fascinated with the new site and the

layout for our assembly work, and I am not surprised the council are going to put a zebra crossing on the road opposite, bearing in mind this will give visitors to the shops here direct and safe access to the council car park behind our new site. It seems to me with the right signs and window display we, that is to say, you Frank could gain more business from the arrangements."

Frank cleared his throat.

"Well I am not quite clear what you have in mind Alice, do you mind explaining in a little more detail please."

"Well, when the council's sign for the car park goes up on our wall, we could put one large red arrow below with the company name on it, suggesting it's our car park, and if we put a selection of those small gilded picture frames and desk mirrors in the window at attractive prices. You know the ones that went so well at Christmas. I am sure all the people going past us to and from the car park would see what we were offering and I'm sure one or two passers-by might come in for a bigger mirror once they visited the shop."

Frank stared at Alice.

"Where did these ideas, these great ideas come from? I mean what was it you did at Uni?"

"Oh no I was just enjoying a couple of years before I started work, thanks to you, but my grandfather was a butcher and when I was a kid I used to help him in the shop and he told me.

'Always set your stall for the customers in front of you and separate the emotions from the facts when you are thinking about attracting new business.'

"He was always telling me I had to work towards my own business."

Frank smiled at Alice and in a more relaxed voice said.

"Well, Alice, you can tell your grandfather you have made a big step towards your objectives today, and for as long as you're working in my company, I shall be discussing the options with you."

Recruiting the CEO

Three men sat around the table, looking at George Hill as he explained his decision and the discussion he had just had with the company's owners. Their expressions mirrored their concerns and anxieties as the changes they were about to face dawned upon them.

"Our owners have accepted my decision to retire a little early, understanding it will improve the opportunity of A1 Connectors to retain the Wargan contract with the Germans if the contract is renegotiated with a new CEO in place who will be properly looking forward to the long term managing and development of this critical trade agreement for A1.

"I realise this decision comes as a surprise to you all, coming as it does six months before my official retirement date but I decided that my decision is in the best interests of the company and you, the Board."

At this point George Hill stopped and looked at his directors as they began to recover their equilibrium.

Finally, Michael Wells his long-time colleague and Finance Director said.

"This is a real shock George and a bother. I mean are we going to find your replacement or are we going to have someone brought in by the Group?"

"No, Group were quite specific on that point. They want you to use a recruitment agency. They are suggesting a company they use but you three will have to make the choice of who is going to move the company on and of course ensure we get the Wargan contract. A1 is trading in great shape as you know, and I am due some back leave so as of the first of next month I am going off to visit my family in Australia, which means I will be out of your hair for a month and that should give you enough time to choose a new CEO. After all this will be a very attractive proposition for somebody with a background in the electrical connector manufacturing business, who will know something of our ability but bring some additional experience to us to supplement your abilities."

"Now, I am arranging a little celebratory dinner for you and your wives at the Bell and Whistle for tomorrow night. I hope you can make it as we look to yours and A1's future. Michael, could you hang on just a moment?"

Once they were on their own George said.

"Look I really want to apologise for not discussing my decision with you but to be honest I have been so stressed recently about the pressure the Group has been putting me under to get the Wargan contract, and at my age I just decided they were just as likely to retire me early, on their terms, and bring in one of their Admin Managers to tell us what to do, and so in the last few days I decided I had had enough.... Sorry."

Twenty minutes later, Michael Wells was back in his office, the door firmly shut, as he unloaded his concerns to the Personnel Manager, Millie.

"No mention of his plans to me until today, when you think how long we have worked together! I mean building this bloody business up and now at a crucial moment he takes his money and runs. I'm sorry Millie I am really upset and shocked about all this and now we will have to sort out a new CEO and the gods only know how difficult this is going to be."

Shaking his head Michael sat down behind his desk as he went on.

"Well I have the name of the recruitment company the Group think we could use.

Target Recruitment. Perhaps you could look them up before I give them a call so I have some background."

Millie nodded and replied.

"Do you want me to call our usual recruitment people any way, Michael, to widen the net a bit?"

"Well best not," said Michael.

"The last thing we want is to get the owners upset at this point and we are going to have to concentrate upon the Wargan contract negotiations because if we lose that we are going to be thirty percent light in our turnover next year, and on

present figures that will be very nearly forty percent of our trading profit, and Millie you know from the work we were doing to calculate the downside of not getting the Wargan contract renewed, we would have to let go at least thirty part and full time staff."

Michael looked up at the Personnel Manager.

"Sorry, Millie, to share this gloomy picture with you which we obviously have to keep to ourselves, although I expect the company will work out something is going on when George does go off to Australia.

We really are going to have to decide when to announce that he is retiring and we are recruiting a new CEO. I'm not looking forward to the next three months and look I need you to be my eyes and ears about the place as I concentrate upon this recruitment programme. Millie, could you get me Gerald Worcester at the owners' office? I have always felt I can trust him and he may be able to give us a bit more background from their point of view."

Later he briefed his two co-directors.

"Gerald was obviously fully briefed by the Chairman, and he seemed only interested in letting us make the selection from the candidates thrown up by Target as long as we arrange for the Group to see the final two before we make our choice. He did go on a bit about the importance of us nailing the continuation contract with Wargan, as if we didn't know how bloody important that is!"

Whilst the three of them were reviving themselves over a cup of tea, a Secretary brought in the news that the liaison Director for Wargan, Wolfgang Stingel, was planning to come over from Hamburg on Thursday to talk through the new contract.

The Secretary read from the email that he understood George Hill would not be present but had explained his reasons for not being about and Wolfgang would like to agree a programme of action with the Directors.

The meeting on Thursday was somewhat strained, despite Wolfgang Stingel congratulating the directors over the year's performance figures. The tension was increased when he reminded the directors that it was a contractual obligation at the end of their five-year contract that the next contract had to be offered to the highest bidding distributor for Wargan's sprung loaded terminal blocks to service the United Kingdom market.

The formal Wargan message delivered, the German reverted to his usual urbane and convivial self, saying.

"A1 has done a good job over the previous twelve months, in particular bringing in the contract they had won with Case Tractors, thanks," said Wolfgang, "to Richard, your excellent Design Engineer. It is the most profitable and certainly has the most potential of any programme for the Wargan product range at this time."

A few days later, Michael Wells had a meeting with a Manager for Target Recruitment which was informative, as he took pains to explain to the other two directors.

"Mainly," he said, "because of the amount of information they already had on A1 Connectors."

A clear indication, they all agreed, that the Group were pulling the recruitment 'strings' behind the scene.

Having little alternative the three agreed they would have to go along with the recruitment strategy Target proposed, where they would be required to interview several candidates, selecting the top two. The two would then spend a day visiting the company with time in all the key departments to get, as the Target representative said, '*a real feel for the company*', before their final interview with Target. The Board would then be given a full evaluation schedule for each of the applicants and the Board could then make their final judgement on their choice of the new CEO.

"All tight and tidy," said Michael, "except we know that Group are keeping a close eye on the project and goodness knows how they will try to influence our choice, but you can bet they will."

The Wargan programme, in preparation for the submission for the next five-year contract, was gathering pace with the product line management team led by their very able Sales and Marketing Manager, Paul, feeding his knowledge of the key accounts and their projections for sales in the year ahead.

Finance were hard at work modelling the cash flow covering all aspects of stock holding and purchase and the levels of sales and service support likely to be required.

The figures the directors decided were looking very solid and even when Michael Wells handsomely discounted the figures for safety, still showed a steady pattern of growth in all the product lines and the project benefits both to A1 Connectors and to Wargan in Hamburg. Figures, the directors comforted themselves with, by feeling that they should be offered the new contract.

The new CEO selection process also moved on, although only three potential CEO candidates were presented by Target for consideration the Board.

On the face of it both of the men and a lady had the necessary technical background and experience in interconnecting component manufacturing on their CVs.

Michael Wells bustled into the HR office.

"Millie, I wonder if you would go down to reception. The two CEO candidates from Target are here for their 'get to know the company day' and I think it better the directors and I do not meet them until they have completed the tour schedule.

Now, Millie, if you could keep a careful eye on their progress, and by that I mean they are kept to the time schedule we have agreed with all the section heads with whom they are spending time. Oh, and Millie, don't mind popping in on them when they are in the departments. It will slow down one or two of the department heads talking too much. After all, they are bound to want to impress the next CEO with their copious knowledge and great managerial skill… if only!"

Millie found the two candidates as the only residents in reception and discovered from a rather flustered Annabelle at the desk that the tall, balding, rather academic one was a Mr Terry Herbert from Target, whilst the younger, good looking one in a very together suit was Chris Dean, also from Target.

Millie welcomed them and took them into the boardroom where tea and coffee had been arranged. She explained that the three directors would be meeting them individually after they had their tour.

Chris asked most of the questions and went out of his way to be courteous to Millie and to claim how helpful this 'get to know you tour' was going to be. He also explained his background was more commercial and he was most interested in that aspect of A1 Connectors before he met the directors.

Terry Herbert's far less informative comments suggested a general management background.

"Just interested to get a feel of the place," was his comment.

Both claimed to know A1 Connectors well from their present roles.

Millie shepherded them off to their allotted slots in the departments and popped in to oversee progress every fifteen minutes.

The difference in style and substance was considerable and whilst Terry Herbert was happy to listen to whatever script he was given, Millie found Chris Dean firing questions, particularly in sales and marketing and in the accounts department, and making notes as he went.

At the end of the organised tour, Millie took them to have a preliminary meeting with the three directors.

Chris Dean was the last to go and coming away from his half hour, well after mid-day, he asked Millie 'if there was a decent pub nearby where he could get a sandwich?'

Quite charmed by his manner, Millie explained there was and when he enquired if she would consider introducing him to the Black Dog and joining him for a sandwich, she happily agreed.

During a convivial and relaxing sandwich and in his case a pint of beer, Chris asked more questions about the comings and goings of the company and the successes the company had enjoyed.

Millie realised several of the questions were related to the Wargan terminal block programme and he was clearly well informed on their range.

Later that afternoon, working on instinct, Millie checked out with Sales and Marketing and Finance what kind of questions Chris had been asking and found that much of his questioning had been focused upon the Wargan contract.

The horrified group of directors met with Millie and called the Chairman of their Group to explain what Millie had unearthed.

"Not a candidate for the role of CEO but a spy out to gain as much information as possible before his company put in a competitive bid for the Wargan contract."

The telephone lines buzzed back and forth before a very indignant Group HR Director told Michael Wells that Target Recruitment had been ceremoniously removed from this and any other recruitment job with the Group and could he arrange a local, trusted, agency to undertake the search for a new CEO and when they had made their selection and confirmed it, would he be kind enough to introduce A1's new CEO to the Group Board!

A New Old Career

Mike Baker sat upright in his high backed seat. The Chairman was addressing him and all eyes around the boardroom table were on his face.

"Michael, I am getting good readings about your team's performance and goodness knows the bank can do with all the good news we can gather in this climate."

The Chairman stopped to slowly survey his directors and their direct reports. Several of whom physically shrank back in their padded seats.

"Your director tells me you took the initiative of introducing us to a senior Chinese official at a gathering at the Chinese Legation that you attended when your director was otherwise engaged that evening?"

Mike's director visibly shrank back in his seat as the Chairman continued.

"It is even more important in these constrained times that we take ALL the options available to promote the bank."

The weight the chairman put behind ALL was ominously clear!

"And now, thanks to Michael, we have a visit arranged next week from the London Business Representative of the Chinese Central Business Group, specifically to strengthen the bank's relationship with the Chinese business community." The Chairman looked directly at Mike and said.

"Now, Michael if you spare me half an hour this afternoon, I would like to go through the arrangements with you."

In the corridor outside the boardroom several of Mike's direct report colleagues nudged him with a variety of comments such as.

'You're well in there, Mike'. 'Chairman's blue-eyed boy now'. 'Any chance of getting me into that meeting, my director's giving me grief?'

Mike slumped back in his seat in his cubbyhole of an office.

"Grace, any chance of a cup of tea?" he shouted through the door.

'This is ridiculous' he thought. *'One lousy idea and now I'm going to be accountable for the bank's relationship with the whole Chinese business community; you can be sure it won't satisfy the Chairman however hard I work at it, let alone my director. Why didn't I keep my mouth shut and my head down like everyone else?'*

After eight that evening when he finally returned to his flat in Wimbledon and had the strength to open the mail after Mary had given him a substantial glass of whisky, he discovered a letter from a law firm in Bromley which read.

Dear Mr Baker,

As you know your mother's brother sadly passed away last October and as his lawyer we have now been able to close and distribute his estate as he had instructed.

I am pleased to advise you that your uncle has left the land and property at the junction of Ashburton Road and London Road, Bromley, some fifteen hundred square feet in all, which as you will know was used by your uncle as a stand area for used car sales.

There is a small office on site and despite your uncle's approaches to the Council Planning authorities it seems unlikely that the change of use he envisaged for this site to provide either living or office accommodation will be sanctioned.

The latest accounts for the used car sales business which is operational and employs a salesman and a mechanic shows a very small profit return for the year ending December last.

Part of the inheritance for the site includes the ownership of the Ace Second-hand Car business. Perhaps you could look in at our office at your convenience to sign the necessary papers of transfer.

Yours faithfully,

Mike stared at the light above him as he sat at the kitchen table.

"I have been sent a signal," he announced solemnly to his wife, only slightly influenced by his tiredness and the whisky. "I am going into a new career."

A few days later Mike found himself sitting in the Ace Motors office with a mug of tea and his two employees, both staring at him as if he had dropped in from outer space.

In an attempt to break down the feeling of tension, Mike explained.

"My uncle left me the business and I am sure he wanted me to keep things going. I have given in my notice at the bank where I have been working for some time and should be able to join you in a month's time. I realise the profits we make are a bit thin having gone through the books but," he finished lightly, "with your help and experience I am sure we can make this business tick."

He looked at the impassive faces of his two employees, who regarded him in silence.

Finally, Eddie, whilst looking across at Andy the mechanic, replied.

"Your uncle said there was no chance for this business with five other second-hand car companies in the Borough and he spent his time trying to flog the place to someone as a building site."

Warming to his task Eddie explained.

"See, I'm sixty and he's sixty-two," glancing again at Andy. "We aren't ever going to get another job and we need the minimum rate to keep going. See I've got a wife who isn't much too well and Andy's got three grandkids with no farfer who need school stuff."

Andy was nodding at Eddie's explanation.

"And we were like hoping you would know someone in the Council who would give us a planning change and you would flog the site and Andy and I would get a bit to put by, like what your uncle promised."

There was a long silence whilst Mike pondered upon what he had just heard.

He knew full well he could manage nothing here without the support of these two and their experience. He felt no concern that he had burned his bridges at the bank and he had enough money put aside for a year or so. '*The children's fund*' as his wife regularly reminded him when she came back from one of her regular 'hen' parties! Mike decided upon direct action in these circumstances.

"Well, Eddie, Andy. I assure you I will be honouring my uncle's commitment to you both for your loyal support to him and if we can get a modification to the planning consent on this site and I find a building developer to build here, of course you will both benefit. Now, in the meantime, I can afford not to be a financial burden on the business and other than expenses as my uncle did, we can continue on if you can show me how each of you work and share your experience on dealing with customers, so that I can contribute where I can to keep the business going."

Eddie and Andy grunted their agreement to the arrangement and Mike arranged to come down the following Saturday and every Saturday until he left the bank, and sit in to get a feel of the way the business was run.

As he explained to Mary later.

"Not a very engaging start at Ace Motors as neither of the employees think the business is viable and they were hoping uncle would have flogged the site and they could have some of the proceeds."

Mary did not say *'Waiting to give in your notice after you had taken a look at the business might have been the smart way forward'*, although that was in her mind.

"Never mind, darling, you will find a way of making it work once you have got used to what Eddie and, what's his name, actually do."

"You mean Andy. Yes, I expect so; otherwise I will have to sign up to stack shelves at Sainsbury's. Well at least I won't be killing myself with fifteen hour days in the bank."

Saturday turned out to be something of a surprise and despite finding himself worried about what to wear, open neck/tie? Bright shirt? His jeans? What would a prospective second-hand car purchaser expect?

Mike arrived at eight-thirty to find Eddie wiping over windscreens to remove the dust off passing traffic, whilst Andy was on the lift in the garage section of the building with a Ford, which he explained needed a front wheel bearing and as he explained to Mike.

"You see, Eddie can always push a punter's expectation of value down before we pass over cash for any of these old ladies, once we point out one or two things that are not up to spec or unsafe, and I can then usually put things right cheaply and make a bit more money when we flog her. Trouble is there aren't enough buyers coming here nowadays, although there are always punters bringing their 'pride and joy' wrecks and trying to unload them with us after they have toured the other used car yards."

The month of Saturdays slipped by and Mike found a grasp of the intricacies of used car sales fell into much the same overall framework as banking services with their customers.

This revelation came to him in the bath, soaking his bones after a not very productive day in the rain trying to convince one or two potential customers that the car they were vaguely interested in was an ideal choice for them.

'*Make sure the customer was blinded by the procedures the banking system demanded or on the forecourt the Road Safety system demanded on the vehicle's road worthiness.*

Ensue the list of procedural requirements for those trying to sell their car reduced the customer's assumptions of the value of their asset, a car, or in the bank, some land, a house, or investments in which borrowing was required and then encourage the potential customer on the forecourt or in the bank, a belief that appreciation was a natural course of events for their financial commitment!'

Hard and not very productive as his involvement at Ace Motors was, Mike enjoyed his new experience helped by the rather cynical, if experienced, advice from Andy and Eddy who had clearly come to the decision that if they were ever going to see a 'pension' fund of any sort, it had to be thanks to Mike's management of the car sales company.

Slowly the number of Morris Minors, Peugeot 305s, 50,000 mile Minis, Transit vans and a slightly damaged Austin Montego Estate came on to the forecourt over the next month and several of them even more slowly found their way, after interminable haggling, into a new home.

The turning point came on a wet miserable Tuesday afternoon after Mike spent a stressful morning trying to put together a financial performance schedule covering the last three months trading for a bank meeting demanded by the company's bank's Area Business Manager, and as Mike full well knew, would expect an explanation of the way the account was constantly drifting over its overdraft ceiling. In whatever way he juggled the figures he was forced to recognise the fact, the site and trading outgoings were clearly exceeding the meagre incomings. A situation that even the dimmest business manager was going to spot immediately!

The small office door burst open and a rather overweight, sandy haired, young man came in, shaking water from his expensive country casual raincoat.

"What a day, can you believe this weather. Jeremy Smyth's the name."

He proffered his hand, gold Rolex and all, to Mike who found his hand being firmly pumped.

"May I sit down?" enquired Jeremy, who had already seated himself in the elderly swivel chair opposite Mike's desk.

"Would you be Mike Baker?"

The visitor did not wait for a response and Mike was too surprised by the larger than life arrival, nothing like any of his normal customers, to make any response.

"I was recommended to come and see you by an old chum of mine who knew you from the bank, Charles Howe. Said you had gone into the motor trade and I see he was spot on."

"Well, Mike," said Jeremy, leaning his elbows on the desk and dripping water as he did so.

"I am in a bit of a bind and I'm hoping you can help. I have a Lamborghini Espada that a dear old uncle of mine has just left me in his will. Now, I am a pony man, these classic cars mean nothing to me and in any case I gave my word I would unload the old lady and pass the bazooka back to my elderly aunt, who I assure you does not want for a bob or two. So when Charlie recommended you as an honest broker, I came here rather than try out any of these dodgy second-hand dealers in the town."

Mike managed to get a foothold into the conversation.

"Well, Jeremy, as you can see," and he swept his arm towards the window. "We specialise in rather more modern used motors and are not really organised in a way to purchase an expensive classic."

"No, no, you don't understand. I don't need you to buy the car but if you could park it on your site, people passing down the London Road would get a fine view of her and someone is bound to come in and make you an offer. Now whatever you think she is worth and you could get, and I mean 'whatever', you get, let's say, thirty per cent of the take, plus expenses, you know, ads, etc., you had incurred. She's been fully maintained and I have all the supporting paperwork and if you agree I could drop her in tomorrow with a letter of agreement on the points I have offered. Only I have to leave for three months in California with a mate of mine working with the Geezers over there and I have just got to get the old lady, that is the motor, off my hands as I promised my uncle, before I go. Will you help me out?"

It only took a second and Mike shook hands once again completely bemused by events as Jeremy left with a, "Great, great, so relieved."

"I will be here at 9.00 a.m. tomorrow with papers and car and with details of my aunt's lawyers to whom you can send the cheque when you find someone. I am so grateful for your help. You have got me out of a real hole and remember whatever you feel is a reasonable price, is the car's price."

When he had gathered his wits together after the surprising visitor, Mike called in his two trusted henchmen and ran through the meeting.

Eddie finally said.

"But we don't know anything about a Lamborghini Espada, let alone one built in nineteen sixty-nine."

"Well," replied Mike firmly. "We are now going to find out what we can on the Web because if we could make the project work, we might save the company and yours and my hopes for the future, bearing in mind where we are now and my impending meeting with the bank.

Half an hour later on looking up information on the Internet, it was clear to all three of them that the Lamborghini and its more than 300 horsepower, that the average price for this particular model, even in modest condition, was over one hundred thousand pounds!

Good to his word, with a taxi in tow, Jeremy arrived in the silver blue immaculate Espada with a signed agreement and a thick batch of papers related to its history, and with scarcely time to say goodbye he was gone on his trip to the USA.

"Right, boys, let's clear the corner right by the road. I have decided our price is £100,000. If we get that over the next month it will be a better return than the sale of every Ford van, Morris and Nissan we have shifted in the last six months."

A week later the deal was consummated with a gentleman whose only comment was, "I have seen the Espada every day this week on my way to the station for London. Could not believe it. I have always wanted one and at this price I want it before someone else snaps it up."

The following Saturday the Chairman of the local Classic Car Club drove into the forecourt in his Bentley and told Mike.

"I see you have gone into classics. Would you have space for three or four motors as the location would show off the classics beautifully and of course the cars could be left under your suggested financial arrangements which would be fine? A good many of our members get involved in a classic motor without too much thought and then they get busy, or the wife complains, and they want to unload as soon as possible.

If you agree I will circulate our arrangement to our two hundred members on Monday."

Mike sat in the office with Andy and Eddie and a mug of tea.

"Here you are, boys, brand new overalls with Ace Classic Cars on the front and back. I am putting all this clutter of crappy motors on to Auction as soon as I can because we have moved into a brand new, well… brand old business, and I'm looking forward to explaining our new business plans to that pompous bank business manager!"

The Joint Enterprise

It was not often that Andrew Bennett was pleasantly surprised by events that had been stimulated by his PR and Publicity company but as he explained to his senior operations team at their Monday morning briefing, the amount of cover the weekend nationals had given the article they had released and promoted on behalf of the Longer Life Foundation, was well and above any expectation he had before the event.

A situation that was mirrored in the faces of his management group around the table!

"I should think the Longer Life people will be well pleased and I feel sure they will now commission us for more cover on the same theme which is why I suggest, Peggy, you brush up on that series of articles you researched on the changes needed to UK pension laws and John that interesting article you did on people facing up to multi-stage life now we are all going to live longer, could you dust that off, and bring it up to date please. Who knows we might get a call for a little academic reflection on the need to face the changes that expectation of a longer life are going to bring to those keen to maintain standards into their nineties, or I suppose even their hundreds!

"Sarah, as you are our medical genius, perhaps you could gather anything you think might help on keeping the body and soul together over a longer lifespan.

"I have a feeling we might strike gold here if we focus on the subject and bearing in mind our somewhat precarious financial situation, get some group or other to use our expertise by presenting arguments that need to be aired and debated by our politicians. Not that they will pay much attention unless there are votes in it. Ok, let's go to it. Your ideas at our Friday meeting please."

Only two weeks later Andrew announced…

"Whilst I am encouraged by the live cover we are getting in the nationals and the reprint fees we are picking up, we are in danger of committing too much of our creative time to the long life subject and I don't have to remind you our 'bread and butter' comes from rather more mundane promotion of business news for our rather too small group of business customers. God preserve them, and this speculative article promotion is, I suspect, more financially rewarding to companies who have products and potions that they can flog to the gullible who suddenly hear they can now live for ever!"

A matter of an hour after the briefing meeting, a call was put through to Andrew's office.

"Good morning may I introduce myself, Mr Bennett, my name is Andre Bozzo. I represent the Swiss Investment House, RS Investment Advisors Group which you may know has interests in financial service companies throughout the European Union (EU), offering financial investment services.

We have been very interested in the informative technical articles you have been promoting recently and I wonder if you could spare me an hour or so when I am in London next week as my group has a project that might interest your company?"

An arrangement was made and Andrew started to find out as much as he could about the shadowy Swiss business, RS Investment Advisory Group.

The Internet showed that a group of consultants and technical advisers based in several EU countries were associated with the RS Security Group offering a range of financial support to investment companies and wealthy individuals.

Andrew decided he would wait until he had his face-to-face meeting before he delved deeper. In the meantime, he drew up a detailed list of his own team's skills in experiences in dealing with matters which might be characterised as supporting a longer life.

The meeting was arranged to be held at the Hilton Hotel in Park Lane where, Andre Bozzo told Andrew, in impeccable English with just a trace of mid-European accent, he retained a suite, as he was such a regular visitor from Geneva to London.

Andre, as he insisted on being called, was a well-dressed, well barbered and manicured slim man in his middle years with all the accoutrements of success about his person from his gold pen and cufflinks to his Rolex watch and crocodile skin wallet, from which he produced an elaborate visiting card with a series of initials after his name which while impressive, were not recognised by Andrew.

"It really is most kind of you to find the time to discuss this little project my company has in mind. I hope you will not mind if we keep our discussions completely confidential. Members of my board are very anxious to promote the concept and we do understand you may not wish to take on the programme when we would of course be forced to seek other sources."

"Oh quite I understand the need for confidentiality," Andrew quickly responded.

"If I may," said Andre, "I will outline the concept my board and advisory team have in mind for you to consider and of course I will be happy to respond to any questions you may have."

Andrew nodded his agreement.

"We are proposing to invest in an informative book aimed at financially well established companies in the UK and EU working with people of means, who are beginning to be aware of the advantages of new planning in financial matters for themselves, their partners, wives and children to deal with the expected extension in life expectancy. I am sure this means you and me, Andrew. It is clear you are in very good shape."

They both laughed companionably.

"We have decided to invest in a publicity book, a readable informative book of featured articles which would interest those considering the implications of a longer life for them and their families.

One of my people brought your articles to our attention and we felt your well-informed and presented ideas would be ideal for such a programme, hence our discussion today. We have decided the English speaking version of 200,000 copies should be distributed through our network, to be followed by a French, German and Spanish release."

Andrew sat back, holding his breath.

"If you bear with me, Andrew, I will give you our financial ideas for the programme as the tax advantages to my group are very important indeed."

Drinks and elegant nibbles arrived in the suite at the push of a button and Andrew was impressed to see Andre Bozzo drop a twenty pound note as a tip into the waiter's tray.

Catching his eye, Andre said to Andrew.

"I always tip big in this place as it helps to ensure I always get the best service."

"Oh of course," said Andrew anxious to give the impression he operated along the same lines.

"Well now, Andrew, I would love to take you to my favourite restaurant for dinner but I have to take my flight back to Barcelona this afternoon. So if you don't mind I will just run through our proposed new company which I hope you will see as a joint enterprise.

"Now my advisory and tax people are suggesting the formation of a new company here in the UK. Your choice of name but something along the lines of 'Longer Life Advice' theme would be appropriate. We at RS Financial Services would use this account to finance the book and to do so we will transfer twice what you feel is necessary as a working fund into a new account, which for convenience I suggest should be with your existing bank, that I understand is HSBC?

"Now, subject to you letting me know your cost for producing the 200,000 English version of the first book we are proposing a 30% margin over your proposed costs, the cost and margin to be transferred to the new joint company. Oh, incidentally we feel a fee to your technical team who have done the work on the articles you have already presented, say £500 per day, to cover the work they have done would be in order, if you agree?"

Andrew could only nod an agreement.

"Now Andrew, if you and your people are comfortable with these suggestions and you could confirm your ball park figure for producing the book and the costs to date, my people thought a new account fund of £10,000 to get things going for the book might be the sort of figure."

Andrew took a heavy pull on his whisky and water!

"Now, my group will transfer £20,000 into the new account which will cover your expenses and margins and be a start-up fund for the promotional activity we will be engaged in the first phase."

Andre continued his lengthy explanation as Andrew sat watching this most sophisticated businessman.

"Now here I have the very best Swiss advisers to ensure we keep everything both in Switzerland and the UK strictly legal. Incidentally I will make sure you get all the advice which I suggest will help minimise tax payments for your own company. I will, of course, get my people to give you the full brief on the tax arrangements, but in principle we need to get the new company in HSBC your present bank, up and operational. Transfer the basic working fund into it and draw your working cheques for the project from the new account.

"Pay off a few of your people the £500 by cheque, let's say when you have worked out your basic book printing costs using all your existing articles, perhaps £10,000 costs. Let me know and I will be arranging our contribution to match that plus 30% into the new account. My people are insistent that the sooner the new account can be shown to be working, however small your initial withdrawals, we can put in place the very important tax easement arrangements in Geneva.

"Andrew, can I assume you are still interested and prepared to go into partnership?"

"Yes you can indeed, Andre. I have made a note of all the steps we need to take and we have a very good relationship with HSBC so I am sure we can get the new company off the ground with a reasonable working fund. Obviously I will need a written contract of the arrangements from your group and I will despatch the cost estimates and timescales to you tomorrow."

"Well, Andrew in view of your professional interest and the commitment your company has already made to extended life understanding, I presumed to have a draft contract drawn up for your people to consider, and by the way as you can see I have here a copy of all the articles you have produced. Well over half the chapters we need for our book I suggest, and also here is a legal document for our signatures working with the new account when we need to prepare some of the publicity expenses from, of course, the funds we are putting into the new joint account."

With that Andre drew out of his leather folder a formal document explaining.

"I think your bank will find this document appropriate to accept signatures for my group's withdrawals in a month or so when we have the promotion on the way."

And with this he signed his name with a flourish on the bottom of the form. Victor Orben is my highly qualified Swiss accountant as you can see, and of course he and I will sign on behalf of the RS group as he does for all important matters. When you are ready Andrew, perhaps you could send me a copy of your own signing agreement just so we also have a record on our files."

"Well that will be me and my qualified ACA Accountant, John Sutcher," replied Andrew. "I have quite a lot to sort out with my people and I know you have a flight to catch, so I will text and call in the next couple of days." As he waved Andre's card in his hand.

"Yes, of course. Now just one thing in view of your positive support for our joint programme. I will immediately put in hand transfer of funds from our Spanish operation into the new account as soon as you have set things up, in fact made a few of your own withdrawals to pay your people. As soon as this starts you see, Andrew, my people will instigate the tax saving programmes from Geneva which I can assure you, you will be very happy about when you look at the new company balance sheet at the end of the first book.

"Now, I should mention before I leave, I will make the arrangement when I am in Barcelona later to get our initial investment into the new account but inevitably this may take a day or two after you have got the company up and organised with HSBC bank, so we must keep in close touch over the arrangements."

To say there was an atmosphere of excitement in Andrew's office when he recounted the details of his lengthy meeting with Andre Bozzo to Peggy, Sarah and John, would be a serious understatement.

The electric atmosphere punctuated by questions and expressions of delight that the company could be on the brink of such a valuable publishing project with a major Swiss financial group, was something none of them could have ever envisaged and to do so because of work they had instigated and worked on was a real bonus and a boost for their professional self-belief.

"Now, I assume we are all of one mind."

Nodding of heads.

"Ok, let's get going and take advantage of this opportunity. I suggest, subject to any ideas you might have, we call the new company 'Longer Life Support Services'.

More nodding.

"Ok, I will text Andre Bozzo once John you get on to that mate of yours at HSBC with whom you play golf, that there is no other company recorded with that name. Give him the outline of the joint project with RS Investment Group and then work out if we can transfer ten grand into the new account from our reserves and of course confirm you and I will sign and Andre and his accountant, Victor Orben, will be signing for the RS side, and explain about the transfer from Spain from RS. Better not mention the Swiss attention to save tax when the project launches the first book programme in English.

Once you have got everything set up, why you don't use that bright young guy, William, you have in your department. Give him some good practise at getting on with an account project and as I remember it, he takes his finals in a couple of weeks, so he will enjoy the experience and gain some practical knowledge."

Two days later and several text communications with Andre Bozzo to give him the progress in forming the new 'Long Life Support Services' company, ' L.L.S.S.as it was to be known by the business community, all the communications being properly addressed by Andre or his Personal Secretary,

Helga, who seemed to be based in Geneva as Andre travelled around Europe, Andrew was even able to advise that he had signed off one or two minor cheques so that Andre's tax people could put in hand the tax saving programmes that were planned.

Wednesday morning started ordinarily enough with Andrew looking at the mail over his first tea of the morning, when the door flew open and John, papers in hand and white as a sheet, burst in followed by William, Sarah and Peggy.

"I have just had a call from HSBC, will it be alright to transfer out of LLSS to some bank I have never heard of in Moldavia to a RS account under the authority of Andre Bozzo and Victor Orben, nine thousand, six hundred pounds, effectively all the money in the joint account."

"They did what!" Andrew was standing, spilling tea all over his desk. "They've tried to clear us out... we have been scammed!"

Andrew sank back into his seat, all his optimism for a bright new future a pile of smouldering ash.

"Only," said John, "they did not get away with it."

"You mean the funds were not sent to this Moldavian bank?"

"I mean just that, all thanks to William."

"Thanks to William. What, why?"

"Well," said John, hand on William's shoulder. "You remember we decided to give Will the experience of setting up the detail of the new account with HSBC and he did. Thank goodness he used his qualification training to set a limit of draw down from the account to five hundred pounds from both partners' signatures and specified that this needed a written confirmation from the other party. Hence the phone call just now. Firmly denied I may say."

Andrew looked at William with admiration.

"William, you have saved the company. Your professional career is assured in this company and although I had not realised what had been suggested to me, your experience of working in a project that we all now painfully see was an out and out scam and a fraud will in fact be invaluable to you, as the bitter experience has been to me."

A Career Move

"I cannot believe it you have been made redundant now!"

The explosion of disbelief practically rattled the kitchen windows and the cat retreated into its basket.

"You're damn near forty. They cannot make you redundant from that bloody bank."

Victoria stood arms akimbo, implacable as ever in her business suit glowering through her heavy framed designer glasses at Nigel, as he sat on the kitchen stool.

"We will have to talk about this tonight but this cannot happen. This would be the final straw. Now I have to go, I have a meeting to chair. You better get this matter sorted out, we will discuss it tonight."

And with this ominous threat she was gone.

Nigel sat on the stool until he heard the BMW back out of the garage before he wearily walked over to the kettle to make himself a cup of tea. He reflected however he had played the news the results would have been the same and he felt ashamed how he had kept the news to himself overnight, deliberately giving her little time to react in the morning before she had to leave for her high flying, fast growing, and designer business.

As he sat back with his mug of tea, he settled once again for the fact that he was out of a job he had never liked and a marriage without children which had over ten years disintegrated into a marriage of social convenience and that was now most likely to come to an abrupt end.

Nigel knew Victoria could never accept an out of work husband and she knew better than him his chances of doing another job with enough status to be socially acceptable within Victoria's growing social circle was remote and her reason for retaining a reasonably presentable, if not ambitious, husband who could be passed off as a bank executive, was gone.

'*Why had this situation occurred*' Nigel thought depressingly as he recalled his manager saying yesterday…

"Nigel, the bank is having to close ten percent of its branches nationwide this year in a real push to get our customers into on-line banking, and I am sorry but I have been instructed to cut back on staff and your role on the counter is redundant. Of course you will get a reasonable redundancy package which should cover you for six months whilst you get another job."

The manager continued trying to sound as sympathetic as possible.

"Your pension pot is, of course, maintained and will no doubt grow until you are sixty-five, but there it is, my hands are tied. I'm afraid you will need to clear your desk at the end of the week, sorry."

'*Sorry is the word*' Nigel thought as he considered the 'drift along' role he had comfortably, if not happily, occupied in the local branch of the bank for some ten years.

Scratching the cat's ears as she sat on his lap, the future personally and professionally looked very bleak to him.

A matter of only a month later Nigel sat at the kitchen table looking at the several piles of papers, letters and correspondence that covered the space, thinking. '*All this stuff pretty much covers my month.*'

The significant pile of letters and catalogues of every size and style that Nigel had just readdressed to his wife's company flat where she was now comfortably residing, reminded Nigel of how much of the world's forest trees are being sacrificed to the culture of circulating not requested, nor read, promotions and advertising mail.

The sale details and the authority to sell the flat with the yellow stickers identifying where his wife's lawyers required him to sign and return to them so that the flat sale could be acted upon swiftly, and rather insensitively, Nigel thought, a draft document on the formal process to end the marriage '*by mutual consent*' had also arrived on the same day.

Bills and accounts that Victoria had always dealt with in her efficient way now littered the table in the same way as the kitchen had developed an untidiness without Victoria's presence.

Nigel looked at the filed marked 'Potential Jobs' filled with newspaper cuttings and agency circulars and the one marked 'Rejections' with, and he reached forward and counted seven letters of regret without, he acknowledged depressingly, a single interview being offered.

"You'll have no problem getting a clerical administrative role after ten years' service here at the bank," said the visiting Personnel Manager heartily on Nigel's last day, "and we will of course give you a very fair reference for any job you like the look of."

'*If only*' thought Nigel.

Whilst he had been surveying on the kitchen table the wreckage of his thirty-ninth year, he had been fingering a pink envelope addressed to him with the unmistakable handwriting of his mother, putting off for as long as possible the moment of opening it, well aware of its theme and direction.

Nigel recalled vividly his conversation a few days after he had been told of the role of redundancy from the bank coming his way.

His mother's indignation over the phone had been principally directed to the fact that Victoria had left him. In her view his loss of this most able and attractive wife was almost on a par to his failure to father grandchildren. '*Her only child depriving his mother of the enjoyment of grandchildren*', as she said.

The fact that Victoria had put her career and company before the inconvenience of having a child had simply not registered with his mother.

According to his mother had he taken on his proper male role and got on with the matter, by now his mother would have at least two grandchildren to love and show to the world!

Her observations over his joblessness seemed to be focused upon how could she explain the situation to the members of the ladies' bridge club to which she belonged, and how like his late father despite all her efforts had never taken his office career seriously, which was why he had left her with such a meagre pension!

The letter proved to be as full of his mother's disappointment as he expected, finishing with the hope his next job would be of the style that she could be proud of.

He wondered idly if stacking shelves in a supermarket would qualify!

Clearing some space on the kitchen table, Nigel decided to write down a list of priorities based upon his early attempts to find a new job.

Top of the list a few minutes later was a 'better CV' and recognising the importance of what skills he had he spent half an hour with the local papers looking, and finding, several companies who were offering professional help to those who were anxious to present themselves to a new employer.

A matter of minutes later he had an appointment that afternoon at the Career Development Foundation, whose offices were less than thirty minutes from the flat.

Arriving in a suit and tie, Nigel was whisked through the impressively modern reception area, despite being twenty minutes early, to meet his Career Advisor, Jane McCall.

"We like people who get early to appointments," were her first words, which Nigel felt was a good start.

He was rather less comfortable after she explained the fee scale for their expertise and help but consoled himself with an *'in for a penny, in for a pound'* thought as she began an interrogation of his background and working experience, continuously typing in the details into her desk computer.

Some of the questions Nigel found difficult to respond to accurately despite the fact that he was determined to be honest in his responses.

'How did he rate his influence on junior members of his team or associates in the bank?'

Try as he might to give a picture, he was forced to acknowledge the bank's personnel procedures and authoritarian way of working scarcely left any space for personal influence over any aspect of the working life.

At the end of an hour's interrogation Miss McCall said that she now had sufficient evidence to gather and shape Nigel's CV and to give him the leads necessary to circulate his CV to potential companies who, she assured him, are looking for people of his age and experience. She did explain this extended part of the service would, "Of course," require additional fees but at this point Nigel was too tired to resist such matters.

Three days later Nigel was back in Miss McCall's office as she explained the details in his draft CV and passed her list of several companies who, "would undoubtedly," be interested in his background and experience.

The, *"Trust us, let's push along,"* process suited Nigel, who skimmed through the official looking CV with his details for a matter of minutes in the waiting room, before confirming his acceptance of the information and agreed to the CV being circulated with, as Miss McCall said '*the priority target being an Administrative Management role.*'

Back in the flat that evening with a copy of his CV and a glass of whisky, Nigel was forced to think through that some of the 'Personal Summary' extended the reality of his banking role somewhat.

One section. '*A highly competent motivated and enthusiastic Administrative Manager with experience as leader of a team in a busy office environment*' seemed a little on the high side to him, although he felt more comfortable with '*Approachable, well presented, able to establish good working relationships with a range of different people*' he felt was not entirely out of order.

The list of Professional Qualifications certainly did not come from his interrogation meeting where his only achievement 'Institute of Bankers Part II' was not mentioned and his new CV claimed NVQ Level II was trumpeted, with a range of management skills this accreditation covered.

'*Oh well*', thought Nigel, '*they must know what they are doing.*'

In the summary of his skills Nigel almost convinced himself, sitting at his kitchen table, that he did indeed have the ability to '*multi-task and manage conflict demands*' and have a '*strong organisational administrative and analytical skills.*' and for the first time for some days he went to bed and slept soundly through the night.

Two days later a request to come for an interview in a food processing and distribution company for an Office Administrative Manager in the town arrived, and suited and booted Nigel presented himself at reception to see the Personnel Director.

The interview seemed to go well as Nigel considered it later, until the point where he had to admit that he had no knowledge of Microsoft Office software at which point the interview went downhill. Which Nigel through might have been just as well as he realised he had rather glossed over the truth in regard to several management aspects of his previous office experience.

Over the next three weeks several interviews came and went without Nigel being called back from any of them.

The review with Miss McCall was clearly designed to prop up his confidence and as he thought about it, no doubt to ensure he continued to reach into his pocket for the service charges.

The change of interview direction came quite unexpectedly when he received an early morning call for an interview to an engineering company some distance away.

Having overslept, without breakfast and tieless, he arrived rather later than the required time in the small rather scruffy company reception office, to find it empty.

Conscious that he had not shaved, he sat down without attempting to find anyone about in the company.

Moments later the telephone on the reception table rang and Nigel decided it might be about his interview and so he rather tentatively answered it.

"Hallo," to which the brisk male response was.

"Oh, you're there. Come up to the third floor office, number five," and the phone went dead.

Apart from thinking this was an odd, if not impolite way to greet an interviewee, Nigel made his way through the internal door that led on to a set of stairs, which he walked up and to the clearly marked Floor 3. He proceeded down the corridor until he came to door number five.

Nigel was about to enter when a harassed looking secretary with a pile of files in her arms came out.

"Thank goodness you are here. We're having such a day. Here is the file, the project group will be in seven, that's just down there. She inclined her head.

"You have ten minutes to glance through the details." This said she thrust a slim folder into Nigel's hands.

"Sit in my office to take a look and then go down to number seven. Just do what you can. The boss is spitting blood about the lack of action. Sorry I have to go, good luck."

And with this she was gone, clattering down the corridor in her high heels.

Nigel sat in her office deciding that whilst this was a form of interview test he had not experienced before, it could scarcely go worse than all the others and at least a live working project might give him an opportunity to actually show one or two of his skills he had picked up in the bank.

The file simply had a sheet of notes about an office reorganisation and a flow chart which demonstrated the way the work moved desk to desk in the office. Details of the sort the bank organisation and efficiency management team were all too enthusiastic about circulating to the branch.

Nigel found three young men sitting in room seven, who all got up to pump his hand with a '*thank goodness you have got here*' comments and '*now you are here please help us sort this problem out.*'

Although somewhat daunted by the new form of interview test, Nigel felt himself warm to the situation and at ease working with the three, one of whom claimed to be an engineering apprentice and the other two engineer trainees working in sales.

In no time at all Nigel found himself in a sizeable office where it appeared a new computer unit had been installed and various desks were cluttered about as a result.

Nigel threw himself into the interview test and with the help of the three lads had very soon sorted the desks with their identified responsibility into a pattern which would allow the paperwork to flow into the authorising manager's office for action.

The apprentice had just found mugs of tea for all four of them and Nigel was wondering when he would be seeing someone about his interview test, when the office door burst open and a man appeared whose importance was clear to the three employees who all promptly jumped up upon his arrival.

The man looked about.

"Thank goodness, the restructuring has been sorted. The sales people have to be in place tomorrow when the computer goes 'Live'. Now you are Mr Briggs, the Time Management chap we have been expecting for several days. John Fortescue, the CEO."

And with this said, Mr Fortescue gripped Nigel's hand firmly.

"Well, no, I'm Nigel Shaw. I was sent here by the Career Development Foundation for an interview for a position as an Administrative Manager and somehow I got caught up in helping these chaps." Nigel finished lamely.

"Good grief," the CEO said. "What a mess. We placed that job last week but thank goodness you stepped in to help out. Was Nigel good, chaps?"

"Absolutely," was the united response.

"Well I have been saying for some time we need a flexible experienced Project Manager to help the fifty or so young engineers with all sorts of tasks our growing company needs. Would you consider taking on the role?"

"I would, sir, very much."

"Good, come up to my office. The HR Director and I will sort out all the details for you. Welcome aboard Nigel."

A New Employee

Barbie carried in the parcel of colourful leaflets promoting the range of Low Calorie Horse Feed to suit those animals prone to laminitis dumping the heavy parcel on the receptionist's desk with a, "I shouldn't be doing this," sigh.

"Morning Barbie – more weight training I see," was the comment from the receptionist who did not look up from her computer.

"Daisy is expecting you. You know your way up," as the receptionist continued to be riveted to the screen.

'No doubt' thought Barbie *'communicating with her boyfriend!'*

Knocking on the door at the top of the stairs, Barbie had the door half open before she heard Daisy Parker call her in.

"Morning, Barbie, got those leaflets for us yet?"

"They are with that new receptionist girl. They look quite eye catching, I hope you will like them."

This said she produced an example from her folder, which Daisy carefully studied.

"Yep, I think we nailed the point on this one. There is a hell of a lot of laminitis about and this feed really works. I am hopeful the distribution through the county in the local rag will get our service across. If so, I'm going to use more of this way to get our advisory services for ponies, support equipment, etc., out to our customers, or better still, new customers. Do you want a cup of tea?"

"Thanks would love one. I'm worn out trying to keep up with the two boys and their football training and school work, now they are in their teens. You wait when your girls get to that age, it's frightening how much more work and time you have to put in to keep pace, and without support we have to take on the whole load, willie nilly! You at least have your company as a platform. I have to get my meagre income from the miserable publicity company who constantly try to squeeze more work out of me for the lowest return possible, but what options have I got?"

They both sat drinking their tea sharing their load as single Mums, commenting as they often did about the weight of their everyday activity demanding a large part of their attention as their growing children's demands increased.

Daisy Parker finally said.

"Between us, I have had a nasty shock this morning."

This said she picked up a letter from the pile in front of her.

"This," she said waving the letter at Barbie, "is a letter from poor old Douglas' Solicitors, you might remember I told you he had passed away a couple of months ago. Well what I didn't tell you, is he loaned me the funds to get my 'Find Pony Equipment' company going. I could never have afforded to get the computer equipment and get things set up without his backing five years ago. Also he only asked me to pay interest at the going bank rate on the loan and that I could manage for the last five years."

Daisy took a sip of her tea and carried on.

"Now according to this letter his estate is demanding a schedule for return of the capital as apparently the contract I signed with the old boy stipulates his estate will require repayment on his death, but honestly I never gave the matter any thought. We are only just keeping in profit now, thanks to the staff costs and the retraining with the wretched level of staff turnover I have to put up with."

Barbie replied.

"Well I have thought once or twice I never seem to see the same girls in the office one month to another. Why is that? Aren't you paying enough?"

"Well I pay the going rate and we do a good job of training because it's quite complicated to make sure the girls all know how to dig out the options for, you know, test and results for worm count on pony's for liver fluke, saliva tests for tape worm, Lycra hoods and tail bags. The hundreds of bits and pieces and services pony owners need to keep their animals on the top line. However, when they have been through our training and get three month's experience, they all seem to want to apply for jobs posted in 'Horse and Hound' and are snapped up for better money, as well as getting a job where they can get independent and move away from home, which also seems to be an attraction. Anyway the costs of labour and recruitment is tipping us into the red and now this letter. Between you and I Barbie, what with one thing and another I am beginning to think I will have to close the company, at least I would have more time for my girls!"

"That would be awful, Daisy, you have worked so hard to make a go of this company. I really know how difficult it is for us single mums but there must be a way of keeping your company going."

Over the next few days Barbie found herself worrying about the news Daisy had given her. Quite apart from losing an important client, her feelings over the somehow unfairness of a good company being forced under began to dominate her thinking.

In the evenings Barbie began to look carefully at Daisy's website, checking her charges against other companies offering the same, or similar, services to horse and pony owners.

Offsetting the boredom of her everyday work, she also checked on to the offered weekly salaries for experienced and new girl employees in similar jobs and even found out property leasing rates for offices of similar size in the area close to Daisy's place.

Barbie enjoyed the exercise which was something quite different for her but although she found that Daisy, as she claimed was paying about the going rate for everything, it clearly was a competitive market and she could quite see how the high turnover of staff was pulling the company down.

On a Saturday afternoon a couple of weeks after her discussion with Daisy, Barbie took herself off to a pony club meeting in the next village.

The event was a new experience for her, practised as she was following the involvement of her two boys regularly in their school and club football games.

Barbie had a plan and quickly found that by posing as a newcomer with a fictitious daughter interested in becoming involved in the pony club, others were open and helpful in giving their advice on all sorts of aspects of keeping a pony and obtaining the right gear and support to do so.

Three of the pony club mothers were even kind enough to invite Barbie to join them with her cup of tea in the tea tent.

The discussion on looking after pre-teenage and teenage children, keeping them engaged both at school and after school activities and managing the household, soon came up and Barbie was interested to find all three wished they had time to take on a job but the nine-to-five demands were impossible for any one of the three to fit in.

Barbie explained that she was able to work, thanks to her children being that little bit older.

Two days later, now with a thought out plan, Barbie was in Daisy's office with a cup of tea. She explained her audit of competitors and then introduced her idea.

"Realising Daisy how your recruitment costs and staff turnover are a burden, I believe there are lots of mums who have had work experience but are now 'pony club mums'. Talking to a few, they would love to be able to go back to work but cannot take on a nine-to-five role."

Barbie continued enthusiastically explaining her proposed plan.

"Now, suppose you were able to offer flexible work contracts for a team of ladies doing say, three or four hours a day, where this fitted into an agreed timescale every day in the week to give you one full nine-to-five cover every working day for each group. They could agree to manage themselves to ensure one of them was on site in the office and because they all begin with real hands-on pony and equipment knowledge their training would only just have to be on using your computer systems."

"I believe these teams of three or four would stay with you and definitely not be looking for new jobs after you had trained them and they would be quite experienced in your market and even bring in new customers, thanks to their pony club connection."

Daisy simply got up and went to give Barbie a hug.

"What a marvellous idea, I'm sure it will work. I will get on to the career advisory people to get an ad out immediately."

"No need," said Barbie, producing a long list of names. "Here are all the names and addresses of the mums in the pony club who live around this area and if you could offer me a job so I can leave the wretched publishers, I will get on to contact and organise the work groups for you so that we can stop this haemorrhaging of cash out of the company and start paying back the loan in a steady way."

Daisy simply said.

"You're hired."

All Sorts of Genius

The HR Director of the bank stood up and took over the microphone, looking down at the upturned expectant faces of fifty of his brightest young middle managers as he adjusted the microphone slowly, and quite unnecessarily, to ensure he had the full attention of his 'flock' at the end of their full day exposure to 'Personal Management Techniques' for those aspiring to the 'Top Job' as the pre-event blurb had put it.

"We are most grateful Paul Blake, indeed indebted, by your wisdom, insight and international experience motivating young managers to develop their skill as early as possible and showing them some of the key areas they should concentrate upon as they make their way forward in this great bank."

He waved his arm towards the dapper man standing to his side who acknowledged in a cultured voice. "Thank you, thank you."

And with this said the director enthusiastically led the round of applause but then held up his hand for silence. The audience responded well and he was pleased to note despite the length of the day's events, his team still gave the impression of keen attention.

"And now our distinguished guest has been kind enough to make a range of his 'Self-Help' development books and videos available for us, and I have tweaked the HR budget." He delayed long enough for a minor twitter from the managers so that he continued. "Each of you can take away a self-help work from Paul's inspirational range."

He continued, "Paul tells me he leaves tonight for a visit to a Middle East Royal Family and then a lecture tour in the United States, so we must not delay him further but I know we all would like a few concluding comments before he takes his leave of us. Paul please, over to you."

"My fellow mind creative thinkers, I know that your illustrious HR Director is determined to continue to involve me by bringing new 'mind developing' techniques into your lives when I return from my trip."

Paul turned to smile at the HR Director, who smiled indulgently back.

"I will be staying with the Royal Family under a programme I have agreed with His Royal Highness to encourage the development of the academic skills of his thirteen children. An important matter in this oil rich state to ensure the royal regime's future is in good hands."

"My tour in the USA is based upon a series of television appearances and the visit to another great bank based in the USA where I will be discussing a long term 'mind development' programme with their senior management for their best up and coming young executives, in much the same way as your own fine bank has been far sighted enough to engage my services to help you gain your full potential.

Paul Blake tidied his notes. "And now I must take my leave of you as I make my way to the airport."

In the limousine Paul closed the glass divide between himself and the driver and called his Secretary on his mobile.

"Gladys, I am on the way to the airport after a tiring day with that tedious HR Director at the bank. Hopefully the rather dull little bunch of young bankers will pick up a range of my products and so my day will not have been entirely wasted. Gladys, send the Director one of the standard 'Thank-you' letters, you know the one highlighting my anticipated pleasure for the follow-up visit. I really do not want to overdo it with this lot… just a couple of visits to push my book and 'self-help' course sales up, should do it!"

As the car sped through the traffic, Paul continued talking to Gladys. "By the way is His Highness sending the official car to collect me at the airport? Oh, good. I'm sure you have notified the quality Press representatives so I get cover when I arrive… Thanks. I like that shot of me getting into the limousine with the Royal flag on the roof."

Two weeks later back from his international tour, Paul regaled his 'team' with the events of his trip, careful to emphasise each incident he saw which might raise his profile as an educational inspiration and leader.

The 'team', as Paul liked to refer to them, consisted of his Accountant, his Hairdresser, a long time and personal friend who had already spent an hour ensuring that Paul's perfectly cut artificially silvered fleeced locks were perfectly gelled, and his PR Agent together with the long-suffering Gladys, his Secretary or his Personal Assistant, depending on events, who spent much of her time sorting out the confusions that Paul's self-interested endeavours were inclined to create.

Gladys had carefully briefed each one of the team to ensure they had the key features that would appear in Paul's over lengthy personal briefing of his royal engagement and US television events, emphasising the educational value and his masterly handling of the trip.

Following regular engagements Paul needed his team's approbation to boost his self-confidence. His team knew from long experience the best way to deal with him was to let him elaborate on what he chose as his successes and then come in with positive comments, invariably suggested by Gladys before the meeting.

Gladys knew Paul needed this debriefing process to bask in the warmth of their admiration and support and he found the discussion often triggered positive and creative spins he could use in later engagements.

Paul was able to detail expansively the attention he had received when training the Royal children and how the Prince, with his Minister of Education, had come into one of his classes with the children and complemented him, emphasising to the children their need for concentration upon the important 'mental literacy' and development programmes and how their English Nanny would help them with their studies when Paul returned to the UK.

Despite the positive spin, Paul's team understood that he would be careful how his Middle Eastern visit was promoted following his last trip to that country, when he had insisted Gladys invite as many of the Press as she could muster to be present on his arrival at the airport, where he had loftily lectured the reporters on his growing 'influence' in the 'forward looking' development of the Middle Eastern states education system, frequently emphasising his own crucial role.

Paul's expected triumph and favourable, if not congratulatory, Press cover was however spoilt by embarrassing questions from several of the Press core as to Paul's reaction to the recent harsh punishment in the oil rich State and the lower levels of education available to girls compared to boys in the State.

The exchange caused Paul to bluster in response and to add to this, one particularly unpleasant reporter had managed to find out under some clause in the 'Freedom of Information Act' that Paul as a UK resident tax payer had an off-shore company which allowed him to shelter revenues generated in the UK from the full burden of the UK tax demands. A scheme that Paul's Accountant had been delighted to unveil to Paul as a, "real tax saving," concept for him, which would add greatly to his income.

Paul neither understood, nor was he in the slightest interested in the technical details of the arrangements and responded to the reporter that his information

"Was almost certainly wrong and in any case when UK leaders in their field, as he was in 'intellectual thinking', should surely be left to benefit as much as possible from the 'sweat of their endeavours'." A phrase he rather liked at the point of delivery!

Unfortunately for his comfort and his Accountant's, this switched the focus of the Press cover to the issue of tax avoidance and to questions as to whether he was considering taking up residence in an 'off-shore tax haven'.

This earlier experience left Gladys in no doubt Paul would require a Press Release lauding his Middle East visit successes, without spending time on the actual details of the visit. She had concentrated on preparing a series of complementary comments, which she rightly thought Paul would like, when she read them from her 'reporter's notebook' at the end of his presentation, giving the impression as she always did, that she had listened intently to his presentation and was reading from his own script rather than concocting them from her knowledge of the detail of his meeting schedules and his ego-driven interests.

At the briefing Paul was a good deal less detailed and forthcoming with his team or Gladys about his much-heralded TV interviews in California.

The main reason for Paul's reticence at the meeting was due to the US publishers who planned his series of TV interviews, not as he wished to promote his US image but specifically to promote his range of 'Mental Self-Help' books, targeted to make sales following the unsuccessful launch of Paul's books the year before.

The Vice-President of Marketing had been very specific in his short meeting arranged before Paul's first 'Face to Face' TV interview.

"Look, Paul boy," said the Vice-President. "You have ten minutes with Rachel Hitch at CWM. She is a 'man-eater' interviewer, believe me, and you are there to push and promote your books, so none of that wishy-washy 'I am a genius' stuff and for god's sake don't mention that middle eastern state trip. She hates the way they deal with their women folk. Get in there and pitch how the Brits' Royal Family use your books. Say something positive like 'The Queen reads a chapter every night before she goes to sleep', no matter what. We need sales here and we need them now!"

Gladys had gathered the gist of the TV debacle from Paul's bitter telephone conversations as he reported how he was, "toured about between TV stations, watched over by one of the VP's marketing thugs".

During the TV interviews Paul fell back on airy platitudes on motivational memory programmes he claimed involvement with which, according to his version, had been frequented by diplomats, business leaders and bankers. Paul knew the interviewer would have no chance of assessing the accuracy of his comments during the interview.

Back at home explaining the 'successes' of his TV interviews, Paul found difficulty and despite giving his team one or two positive comments it became obvious the tour in the USA had not been the success he had anticipated when he left for the trip.

To cheer him up his PR 'Manager' ventured to introduce his book promotion programme for the 'Strength of Verbal Reasoning in the Electronic Age' and Paul's new slim book 'The Potential for Intellectual Control in the Present Dysfunctional World'. Reminding Paul that the publishers in the UK had been led to believe they could use a range of 'positive comments' attributed albeit loosely from leaders of the Confederation of Industries, the Trade Union

Movements and several commercial conglomerates and banks, all promised by Paul at the time he had delivered the script.

"Have you managed," his PR 'Manager' asked cautiously, "to get a couple of comments yet?"

Three days later Gladys called the team into the office where they found Paul slumped in his chair unshaven, grey with fatigue, his bloodshot eyes seeing nothing, as they crowded around filled with anxiety.

Gladys took over events saying abruptly, "The American publishers have pulled all Paul's books and are not publishing or promoting his new book next year. We heard this morning from some 'nobody' in the UK publishers that they had decided to stop publishing or promoting Paul's books following the negative reviews he has had of his TV book promoting interviews in the States and their dislike of his association with the Royals in the Middle East State."

Gladys continued in harsher tones. "We also had a call from the office of the HR Director of the bank to say, in view of the negative media cover of Paul's US trip the bank board had decided not to proceed with his business development programme and are returning the consignment of Paul's books and videos."

There was a silence whilst the team stared at Paul as he slumped further into his seat.

"Well," said Gladys firmly. "You have all lived off Paul's back for the last few years. It's up to you to come up with some ideas on what we do next."

The silence continued whilst everyone continued to stare at the 'Intellectual Genius' almost merging into the grey leather upholstery of his office chair.

Gladys despatched the depressed and silent team on their way with the threat, "that they had better come up with some ideas to save Paul and his reputation, and they better do it soon," before she sent Paul to his bed, in much the same way as she had in days gone by despatching her disobedient schoolboy son to his room with the TV off.

Gladys sat and thought with a tumbler of Paul's good Malt whisky to help her concentrate on the problem.

The second whisky at least provoked positive activity and Gladys started from 'A' looking through her file of more recent visiting cards that Paul had accepted at meetings or visits over the last year in a desperate hope she might find someone who could help Paul.

Gladys reasoned that any contact further back would be unlikely to react positively bearing in mind, as she reasoned, Paul's propensity for upsetting people with the way he underpinned almost all conversations with strangers by indicating, one way or another, he was 'intellectually superior to them' with a deep understanding of the subject, whatever that subject was.

Other than a growing warm alcoholic glow, Gladys had no reaction to the cards she thumbed through until she got to a Michael O'Flannigan.

Michael O'Flannigan, Author with a Dublin address card caught her attention, mainly as she had written on the back of the card, 'Charming – has a nice line in physical self-help books'.

Gladys thumbed the card remembering the personable young man with, as she recalled, three young children as he had proudly showed her their photos. Michael had been most anxious to meet the 'Great man' but Paul, as ever, had no time to give a struggling young writer and Michael had gone on his way.

With no better ideas but an instinctive feel and an alcoholic enthusiasm to ignore risk, Gladys phoned Michael's mobile.

"Hallo Michael, I am just calling as Paul Blake and I have just been discussing your visit and he was saying he was so sorry he had not been able to spend a few minutes with you. How are those 'Self-help your body' books of yours going?"

"Gladys," replied Michael in his gentle Irish accent. "How nice of you to call and how appropriate as I was talking to my publisher only yesterday about the influence of Paul's work on my new book coming out next year, and as it is a bit sensitive I was screwing up my courage to give you a call. I will be in London tomorrow, would you mind if I came down to visit you and perhaps with a bit of your advice, Paul could spend a few minutes with me?"

A day later Michael was sitting in Gladys' office with a cup of tea whilst she looked with interest at his children's photos displayed on his iPhone.

Paul resided in his four-poster bed, as he had for the last two days refusing to take any phone calls, let alone face up to his disintegrating world or anything outside his bedroom, his self-confidence completely shattered.

Michael, fortified with tea and Gladys' friendly interest, asked carefully, "Gladys, may I speak to you in confidence?"

"Of course," Gladys immediately responded. Her impeccable judgement of people told her here was someone she could trust and 'any ship in a storm' in the dire circumstances that Paul was in.

"Well," said Michael, "my publishers have become very excited about an idea I discussed with them a few months ago, and have offered me a significant contract to publish my draft 'Self-help book on Solutions for Insomnia' with more to follow. What I need your advice on is how I should approach Paul?"

"So what has your new book programme got to do with Paul?" asked Gladys.

"Well you see," Michael replied. "I have used several whole chapters of Paul's intellectual and mind development books in my new book and I will need his agreement to publish. My only problem Gladys is how I have used them. You see I found in my research for my book 'Learning how to manage sleep problems and insomnia' that in a trial a whole range of people from various backgrounds and ages really improved their sleep quality by reading something really boring before they tried to sleep, and well frankly, Paul's books filled the bill perfectly."

Gladys stared at Michael. "Oh my goodness," she said.

Michael said quickly. "On the positive side if Paul agrees to have his name on my book as a contributing author with me, his return up-front on the first run in English, and several overseas markets including the USA, would be several thousand pounds and I have given my commitment to have a second book ready for publishing within six months. If Paul agrees for me to use his work in the same way and I'm sure you could expect a financial benefit from working with me for some time, do you think he would agree Gladys?"

Gladys sat back in her chair and smiled.

"Michael, I am impressed and delighted for you. I can assure you Paul will sign today as a supporting contributor for you. After all it will give him a new intellectual challenge, learning how to 'bore people' with intellectual techniques. It's just the sort of boost he needs right now!"

Finding the Way

"Quite honestly Lionel, I really feel you should take the redundancy package. You know the new owners will top up your pension fund because of your thirty years' service and you would never settle in Buffalo out there in the USA, now would you?"

"Well," said Lionel blowing his nose vigorously. "I think it is bloody arrogant to shut us down and move everything to the Buffalo office, when I think of how we have worked so hard to build up the business. Since they bought us out and taken on all their never ending changes my job has been a nightmare, and that cocky Director of Operations, Carl Hammersley, on my back all the time."

"Well, that's it Lionel, as Operations Manager you have had a very difficult two years, now you can afford to do what you want at the age of fifty-nine. I thought you would be pleased and I am sure your wife will be. You know, spend more time at home, little trips, and things like that."

The kitchen door slammed shut.

"I'm sorry this isn't working."

His wife, Hilda, looked over spectacles at Lionel. "You have been mooning around the flat for a month with nobody to boss about, and," she added firmly as she collected the breakfast plates and took them to the sink. "I have decided to go and stay with my sister in Aberystwyth. When I agreed to marry you so soon after your divorce I warned you, you

172

would have to change your ways if our marriage was going to work and we managed when you were working but now you being made redundant, it just emphasises your refusal to adjust to anything that doesn't suit your ways, and so rather than us constantly rowing in the vain hope we find a new happier relationship I am leaving you so that I can get on with my life and hopefully you can find yourself on your own."

Lionel put the 'it could be butter' pack and the marmalade back in the fridge.

"Fine, fine, I will be fine. I like my own company."

And without further ado his wife left the kitchen and went to pack her things.

Harry, the Golf Club Secretary, said, "Could I have a moment Lionel. You know I'm sure, your membership is as a corporate member and as your company, well your old company, has had a change of circumstance well naturally the membership has been cancelled."

He held up his hand. "No I do understand how awkward this is for you and I realise as a regular member playing here you might like to take out a personal membership and, of course, I will be happy to put your name on the waiting list, but I am sure you know we do have quite a few potential members on that list. As we have a full membership, it will take a little time for your request to come up before the Membership Committee."

The Chairman took a glass of water to clear his throat.

"Thank you gentlemen, before I close our business group meeting I am sorry to say after all these years Lionel will be leaving us as his company are relocating to the USA. I am sure Lionel would appreciate a round of applause for his valuable contribution to our administrative matters over the years."

Lionel was sitting in the kitchen with the morning newspaper and his tea and toast when Mrs Barnes came in to put her dusters and the hoover into the cupboard.

173

"Well there you are Mr Purcell, you are all tidy and I have changed your bed sheets for you. Now Mr Barnes has said I have to cut down at my age and I am stopping one or two of my customers, and as, well, you are on your own now and so tidy, you won't miss me not coming in I'm sure."

For the umpteenth time Lionel tried to catch up with what was happening to him and to his lifestyle.

He poured himself another glass of malt whisky as he stared out of the flat window through the teeming rain.

'Why had the normal things in his life all left him, what had he done to deserve this, this being abandoned as if nobody wanted him about as if he had the plague. Have I been mean, horrible, uncaring to people', Lionel thought as he saw his shadowy reflection in the rain swept window and as the whisky took a hold, he acknowledged he had been a bit, well very, bossy at times in the company, with his two wives, and maybe sometimes outside the company. *'Probably'*, he thought now dismally, *'why my first marriage failed, well, I suppose both marriages have failed. If only we had had a family things would be different now.'*

Lionel slumped into his seat.

'If only I hadn't been so sure a child would 'disrupt' our lives 'bound to cause difficulties, schooling and the costs'. Lionel recalled the carefully rehearsed arguments he had given his wife when he had started his career in the company.

Lionel found himself weeping as the enormity of his failures to manage anything except his single-minded determination to control the administrative functions of the old company.

Sitting awkwardly opposite the psychologist who said, "Dr Allgood has been kind enough to give me a full detail on the changed lifestyle you have experienced over the last three months and the effect this has had on you."

She smiled encouragingly at Lionel. "He also advises me," she said, "that you are in good physical condition for your age. Perhaps a little tendency," she went on, shuffling the letter, "to increase your alcoholic intake in the recent period? Now what I am going to prepare is a series of exercises which you can do to help you sleep and relax to give you time to relate to the changes in your life. But what I am going to suggest as a first step is you join my discussion group where we share our experiences to give each other support and encouragement."

The meeting room and the seats were comfortable and the flowers in a pot on the windowsill offered a nice touch, while the automatic tea and coffee dispensing machine and the packets of biscuits, freely available, all suggested that everyone's money had been well spent.

Any feeling of comfort was dispelled as he took in the other members of the 'discussion' group who were draped, lolling or sitting rigidly tense around the table. None of this seemed to bother 'Mary', the psychologist as she smiled and said.

"Now I see everyone has got a drink. Oh, you haven't, Betty. Well there is water, you see there in the bottle."

Mary continued, "Now let's all introduce ourselves. No, I know you have been before Betty but you see Lionel and Marsha have only just joined us. Now could we all just introduce ourselves starting with Piers?"

Piers, in a football shirt, his bulging body expanding over the arms of his chair, scratched his shaven head featured by a strip in the centre left long ago blonde. As he scratched he exposed his podgy arm embellished with tattoos to the point where it would be difficult to find any space to add further decoration. His puffy face was contorted as if in pain.

Finally he said heavily, "I'm a Villa fan," and slopped even further back in his seat in silence.

"Now, Piers," said the psychologist encouragingly. "Tell us where you are living now."

After some thought Piers said, "Living now where the Social give me a room."

"I see," said their leader. "Perhaps, Marsha, you could tell us a bit about yourself."

Marsha took the stage with gusto for the next ten minutes with a graphic disclosure of events from her special needs school and her return with the help of the police when she had 'had enough' and 'went visiting' to places that clearly catered for the sex trade. Her heavily made up features glowed with enthusiasm as she set about describing in some detail her adventures, which certainly caught the attention of the rest of the group until Mary said.

"Well now we must give everyone a turn."

And the meeting fell into a more regular description of the difficulties those struggling with their place in society saw themselves.

Mary had left Lionel until last and having had the time to prepare himself, he adopted his office administrative style to explain he had 'moved out' of his job, without explaining why, and his wife had left him, again without explaining why.

Mary set the group a task of giving their views on a social problem that had been highlighted in the local press and with the help of tea and biscuits, and a bit of guidance from Mary even the taciturn Piers managed a few fairly dysfunctional comments to add to the strange mix.

Lionel found himself quite enjoying the human interchange without feeling really part of it but with the virtual elimination of any other social discussion, he found himself rather looking forward to the exchanges.

In his one to one meeting with Mary, Lionel could now freely admit to her he felt isolated and lonely and without the confidence to join a social group or try to find a job helping, as she had suggested, in a local charity where she suggested he could use his administration skills.

Lionel now realised his focus upon administration skills had got him into the mess he was in and he felt that reapplying his role, even in a charity, would simply isolate him further.

Despite Mary's encouragements, week followed week where the television and newspapers were his primary outlet to the world and his shopping visits to the supermarket to get the basic essentials only required him to exchange the minimum courtesies and very little eye contact.

His isolation was probably not helped by the discussion group where Piers had taken to indicate as often as possible, 'I'm wiv Lionel on this one, he nos wot it's all abat, dun he', thus saving himself the bother of giving the matter any consideration.

Mary did convince Lionel he should try to join the local Literary and Social Club, and arranged an appointment to 'pop in to meet the Secretary.'

At the meeting despite her attempts to interest Lionel in the Club, he found the personal questions about his interests and activities too challenging to follow up.

Lionel realised his life was sliding downwards and in a desperate attempt to keep away from the evening third of a bottle of malt whisky, he decided to redecorate his bedroom.

Pulling out the dressing table into the hall, followed by the chest of drawers and all the loose fittings gave him a sense of purpose he had not felt for three months and black bagging unwanted old socks, nail files and varnish from his departed wife, parcelling up business shirts and ties for the charity bag, further encouraged his endeavours.

It was while he pulled out the lining paper in the top drawer of the chest, he found the letter caught up in the corner. Seeing it addressed to his first wife with a South African stamp and postmark from two years earlier, he slid the single page out of the already opened letter. It read.

Dear Mother,

Although you abandoned me I felt it was important for you to hear I have just given birth to a daughter, your granddaughter.

Now happily married to someone whose family own a successful bakers shop here in the city, I can look back at the advantages I had growing up in the adoption home, giving me strength to deal with my isolation and loneliness.

Florence.

Lionel stared transfixed by the letter and its contents which he read again and again.

The next few days passed for Lionel in a blur of unaccustomed activity. He phoned Mary to say he would not be coming to the group meeting on Wednesday. Indeed he was not sure when he would next see her as he had booked a flight to Port Elizabeth, South Africa, and was in the process of tidying up his arrangements with the bank and flat security as he was going to find his two year old granddaughter.

He explained the letter and Mary's response was to be thrilled about his intended journey.

"You have taken on a really important project. Marvellous, who knows where it will lead you, I'm very proud of you, Lionel. Make sure you keep me posted and I will tell the discussion group about your progress. Sadly Piers will miss you as he really sees you as his role model!"